THE TW
WITH HIS W

Suddenly the door of the room was thrown open and Lieutenant Carter strode in.

"Mr. Car—" Will started to say, but his words were cut off by the riding whip Carter slashed across his face.

Carter turned instantly and brought the whip down on Walt. Meanwhile, Will, recovering, and with blood running down his face, charged. But Carter's fury gave him speed. Sidestepping, he drove his heavy boot into Will's crotch. The boy fell writhing to the floor.

"You filthy swine!" Carter stood over both of them now, his fury giving him unassailable strength. "You can be thankful I don't kill or castrate the both of you!" And he began whipping the two of them again across their backs and buttocks and legs.

Finally the blows ceased. Carter's shoulders relaxed, his eyes filled, and sobbing uncontrollably, he turned and hurried from the room.

It was a long while before Walt spoke. "Christ, I'll kill that sonofabitch," he said.

"Let's get moving," said Will. "Maybe we can kill them all."

EASY COMPANY

EASY COMPANY

AND THE CARDSHARPS

JOHN WESLEY HOWARD

A JOVE BOOK

EASY COMPANY AND THE CARDSHARPS

A Jove book / published by arrangement with
the author

PRINTING HISTORY
Jove edition / July 1982

ISBN: 0-515-06350-9

Jove books are published by Jove Publications, Inc.,
200 Madison Avenue, New York, N.Y. 10016. The words
"A JOVE BOOK" and the "J" with sunburst are trademarks
belonging to Jove Publications, Inc.

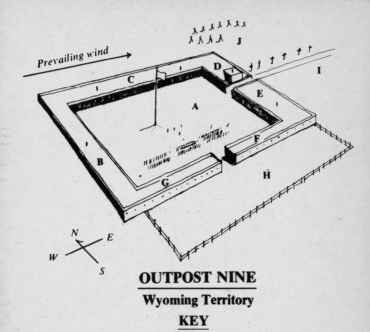

Prevailing wind →

N E W S

OUTPOST NINE
Wyoming Territory
KEY

A. Parade and flagstaff

B. Officers' quarters ("officers' country")

C. Enlisted men's quarters: barracks, day room, and mess

D. Kitchen, quartermaster supplies, ordnance shop, guardhouse

E. Suttler's store and other shops, tack room, and smithy

F. Stables

G. Quarters for dependents and guests; communal kitchen

H. Paddock

I. Road and telegraph line to regimental headquarters

J. Indian camp occupied by transient "friendlies"

INTERIOR   OUTSIDE

OUTPOST NUMBER NINE
(DETAIL)

Outpost Number Nine is a typical High Plains military outpost of the days following the Battle of the Little Big Horn, and is the home of Easy Company. It is not a "fort"; an official fort is the headquarters of a regiment. However, it resembles a fort in its construction.

The birdseye view shows the general layout and orientation of Outpost Number Nine; features are explained in the Key.

The detail shows a cross-section through the outpost's double walls, which ingeniously combine the functions of fortification and shelter.

The walls are constructed of sod, dug from the prairie on which Outpost Number Nine stands, and are sturdy enough to withstand an assault by anything less than artillery. The roof is of log beams covered by planking, tarpaper, and a top layer of sod. It also provides a parapet from which the outpost's defenders can fire down on an attacking force.

one ——————————

On the High Plains of Wyoming Territory, the chill of the early-spring night seemed to intensify as the sky began to lighten for the coming day. Private George Gribble, on his last hour of guard duty at Outpost Number Nine, shook himself, shook away the chill that lay on him like a mantle, shook off his fatigue. Looking now toward the east, he willed that the day come quickly. He longed for a mug of coffee as he started his patrol once again along the east wall by the lookout tower and gate, his heavy feet scuffing on the dull brown sod walkway.

It had been a long night, his first tour of guard duty; still he was eager, not yet jaded from the routine, the boredom, the accumulation of endless days and nights of outpost duty. Young George Gribble had enlisted to fight the Indian. But these were times of peace, albeit a spotty peace; the Custer debacle at the Little Big Horn was still vibrant in the talk of the soldiers who made up the Army of the West. The Indians were on their reservations, the presence of the army reminding everyone—

red and white—that the treaties would be respected. To be sure, there had been sporadic "uprisings," raids on settlers, encroachments on Indian lands by whites, and various infractions of the paper to which the chiefs had applied their mark; but for the most part, peace and boredom reigned. It was certainly so for Easy Company, the detachment of mounted infantry stationed at Outpost Number Nine. And it was most decidedly so for the Sioux, Cheyenne, and Arapaho of the Northern Territory.

Private Gribble looked again toward the east, noting the light slipping along the horizon. It was still hard to see distant objects out toward the deadline. Most of the terrain even closer to the post was as yet undefined.

A light wind stirred then, bringing to him the smell of horses and smoke and—from the kitchen directly beneath his feet—coffee.

Gribble had just concluded another circuit of his post when he experienced a sharp itch in his right armpit and wondered whether his mother's fears could be true: "Those army soldiers never take baths and they all have lice out there on the frontier." Reaching across his body with his free hand—he was holding his Springfield .45-70 rifle with the other—he had just begun to scratch himself when his attention was caught by something just beyond the perimeter of cleared ground around the Post.

Private Gribble stood absolutely still, peering into the gray light, his rifle still on his shoulder. Only there was nothing that he could make out.

But now—over there to his left. Yes, something had moved. Antelope? Coyote? Or was he imagining it?

Gribble shook his head. He knew he was green. Fresh from eastern Pennsylvania, he wasn't even sure of the difference between mounted infantry and cavalry, though he knew there was a difference. But he did know he didn't want to sound a false alarm.

He ran his hand over his face, rubbed his eyes, and

stared again. Nothing. Yet he waited while more of the night receded. He could make out the line of telegraph poles leading eastward down the dirt trail toward regimental headquarters, but not much else. And there again—a movement. Without realizing what he was doing, he brought his rifle down from his shoulder and held it with his finger near, though not actually on the trigger.

Green as he was—not yet twenty—he was shrewd, with the survival instinct of one raised in the streets of an Eastern city. He had no wish to incur a chewing-out from that fire-eating Ben Cohen, who this night just happened to be sergeant of the guard. There—something moving again. It suddenly occurred to Gribble that, hostile or animal—or whatever—it was out of range.

First Sergeant Ben Cohen, on duty as sergeant of the guard, heard the sentry's call, and swore. He had been awake most of the night and his humor was not one that improved through lack of sleep. When he heard Gribble, he had been immersed in making up his duty roster for the coming day, not an easy task since Easy Company was understaffed. Cohen daily regretted his lack of a large list to draw from for certain details, which hampered his maneuverability with the men.

For a big man in his mid-forties, Ben Cohen moved not only quickly but with a force that often surprised his men, even those who had been with him over the years. It was said that the first sergeant was not a man who spent time picking his way around or over a wall, but simply went through it. At the same time, he had a brain that would have earned respect from a Machiavelli. Strength, cunning, and resolve were the qualities with which the acting master sergeant of Easy ruled the company. Before him all enlisted men trembled, and even officers deferred.

3

Only a few moments passed before Cohen bore down on Private Gribble, his face dark with demand. He did not like being called on foolishness, imaginary sightings, or the fears of the uninitiated. Cohen well knew how edgy a green recruit could be in the early hours after a long night on guard, especially on his first tour of guard duty. Half of them wanted to avenge Custer and the Little Big Horn; the other half worried that the Sioux and Cheyenne were feeling their oats over the big Indian victory and, even though peace prevailed in the north, would use the momentum of the Custer massacre to mount a fresh war on the whole territory.

Gribble, still not sure of what he was seeing, felt the lurch in his guts as Cohen, all size and energy, strode onto the parapet.

"Well, Gribble?" When the first sergeant spoke, it always seemed that his voice came from deep inside his bull neck and huge shoulders; someone had once described it as sounding like a rockslide.

"Over there, Sarge. I swear I saw something move. I mean—not just once, but quite a few times." Gribble, a lean man with a long nose, thin hands, and short fingernails, pointed, stumbling over his Pennsylvania accent; yet he was relieved that the first sergeant was there.

Cohen said nothing, only peered in the direction of Gribble's pointing finger. It seemed to the young sentry that a very long moment passed, and he began to feel more nervous about his own first sergeant than about any hostiles that might be out there.

"We'll watch it a minute," Cohen said finally—which, Gribble noted, was just what they had been doing.

"I don't see anything now," the enlisted man said anxiously.

"Stop talking and listen." The sergeant's voice was hard as a shovel, and Gribble felt his face redden.

Cohen was watching him out of the side of his eye,

4

looking for signs of weakness and strength; but he was careful not to let the other know he was being watched. "If you talk," he said, "you can't see so good. Understand?"

"Yeah, sure, Sarge."

Cohen knew he didn't understand, but was too damn nervous to say so. "Let your eyes go soft," he said. "Relax. You can see better that way."

"There!" suddenly burst from Gribble as he pointed.

"I see him," the sergeant's voice was thick with irritation. "I been watching him and that other one there this good while."

Private Gribble stared at him. He had seen nothing until that very moment. "What is it?" he asked. "Is it Indians?"

"It ain't your sweet old Grandma." Sergeant Cohen, feeling the early-morning chill on his shoulders, sniffed and spat vigorously in the direction of his gaze.

When he said nothing further, Gribble repeated, "What is it, Sarge?"

"Look there," Cohen said, nodding just off to Gribble's left.

Gribble saw nothing, and this made him feel even more nervous. Then he did see something move, but he could not distinguish what it was.

"Don't get your bowels in an uproar now," cautioned the sergeant. "Could be they're just farting around a bit." He raised his big head, his eyes suddenly feeling the sky. "It's spring, young feller, and spring's the same for Mr. Lo—the poor Indian—as it is for Lo, the poor soldier. The Sioux get just as horny as we do, by God."

"You mean, they're—they're *screwing* out there?" Gribble's eyes were bugging out of his head; he couldn't believe what he was hearing.

Cohen's big face suddenly broke into a big grin. "I mean they're on the prod. The young bucks. It's spring,

5

they're looking for action. Been cooped up all winter on the reservation, and this time of year they're used to going on a big hunt—lots of action. Except this year they're not; they're stuck on the reservation."

"But what are they doing here? Are they planning to attack the fort?"

"Shit!" The expression on Ben Cohen's face would have withered a side of beef. "Private, this here is *not* a fort, goddammit! I dunno what the hell they teach you recruits these days, but it sure don't have much to do with the army. This here is an outpost and we are a company. A regiment holds down a fort. Got it?"

"Yessir—I mean yes, *Sergeant!*" Gribble was almost falling apart with embarrassment.

Cohen let the roar that was building inside him subside. He said nothing.

"Uh, Sarge . . ."

Cohen looked at Private Gribble in stony silence.

"Sarge, if that is Indians out there, uh—shouldn't we ought to be doing something about it? I mean, like waking everybody?"

"Son, it is Indians. And they are waiting for sunrise."

"You mean the Indians don't fight at night?"

"That is bullshit! I mean, the sun will be up soon and it will be shining right in our eyes. That's when they will attack. *If* they are planning to attack at all."

Now the dawn was opening just behind the horizon, lightening the rest of the sky and the terrain around the post.

"We'll study 'em just a minute or two more," Cohen said. "To make out who they are, what tribe."

"What's that?" Gribble said suddenly, alarmed by a strange sound.

"That?" A grim smile broke on Cohen's face. "Boy, you are sure jumpy. That noise?"

"Yeah, Sarge."

"That, soldier, is my guts rumbling from that swill Sergeant Rothausen served up last night at grub call."

Gribble suddenly felt a laugh bursting inside him, but managed to control his face.

"You keep your eye on 'em," Cohen said, stern as a post. "It'll be sunup soon enough. Try to see where the big clusters are, and who is moving where. And if they move in any closer. They're still out of range. Spot where individuals take cover. Don't let 'em know you've spotted them."

Private Gribble wanted more than anything else to ask Sergeant Cohen to sound the alarm. He was beginning really to sweat with it, as Cohen started to move away, leaving him by himself.

"Stop worrying, young feller. Like I been telling you recruits all these years, you gotta notice things and quit talking so much. Like down there."

Gribble turned to look where the sergeant indicated, seeing now the men quietly hurrying out of the barracks onto the parade.

"On guard duty, soldier, you should know it when the officer of the day is in your area."

"I never saw him, Sarge."

"That's what I know. You were talking and worrying. 'Course, I had you busy looking out there, too, so we'll say no more about it. This time," he added. "Just be glad you got an OD like Lieutenant Kincaid."

Giving a quick tug at his crotch where his longhandle underwear was binding him, First Sergeant Ben Cohen started along the parapet. He had a feeling that Private Gribble would work out all right.

First Lieutenant Matt Kincaid ran the palm of his hand across his tanned, wind-roughened face as, standing in the entrance to the stables, he watched Easy Company's top kick advancing toward him. There was still a sharp

7

coolness lingering in the high mountain air, left by the swiftly departing night, but he knew the day would soon grow warm, and eventually quite hot. He stood there, a tall, muscular man in his thirties, military in bearing, though not rigid, with an easy grace in his stance and in movement too, his faded blue forage uniform fitting him neatly.

He had been in his office when he'd heard the sentry call from the east wall, and going out, he had seen Sergeant Cohen swiftly crossing the parade. Something had called up that familiar uneasiness in him just before Gribble shouted for the sergeant of the guard, and he knew it could be heavy trouble—like Mr. Lo. His suspicions were verified the moment he took a look from the tower over the gate, and he immediately alerted Sergeant Olsen, ordering him to pass the word for a semi-alert to Lieutenant Carter and First Platoon. He considered whether or not to rouse Captain Conway, but decided to wait until he had talked with Cohen and, if he could find him, Windy Mandalian.

Coming up to him, Ben Cohen saluted smartly. Kincaid returned it, and the sergeant plunged right in.

"Lieutenant, there's Oglalla and Hunkpapa just the other side of the deadline, as you more than likely already know."

Kincaid nodded. "They've got the post pretty much surrounded, Sergeant, if not completely. We'll know soon enough when it comes light."

"How many you figure is out there, Lieutenant?"

"Hard to tell. Depends if they're figuring on a full-scale attack, or if they're just a bunch of young bucks looking for a skirmish to count coup."

"They're still out of range, sir."

"Got any notion whose band it is?"

Cohen shook his head. "No sir."

"I've got First Platoon alerted, but I haven't called

8

Captain Conway or any of the platoon officers yet. It could be a social call."

Ben Cohen looked at him wryly. "You don't believe that, do you, sir?"

Matt Kincaid grinned. "I wouldn't put my month's pay on it, Sergeant. But it's good sense to take everything into account. I've seen too many hard johnnies charge into something assuming wrongly that the other one is on the prod."

"True enough, sir. True enough." Cohen paused and then said, "I got a notion they're some randy bucks feeling their oats come spring. Probably want some action so they can count a little coup, get some points."

"Young bucks," Matt said with a sigh. "Sure enough, they're wanting to burst out after being tied down all winter, listening to the old men tell about the Shining Times, with the wars and the buffalo hunt."

"And now they're ready to cozy up to some of those Indian maidens," Cohen said.

"And it's initiation time," Matt added, looking up at the sky.

"Yes, sir. It is that, sir." The first sergeant nodded, pulled up a bit short by the lieutenant's serious demeanor.

"I don't want Mr. Lo to know we've spotted him," Matt said.

"I've warned Gribble about that, Lieutenant."

"He's green. Better send a man up there with him. And where the hell is Windy?"

An innocent look spread over Cohen's face as he spread his palms and shrugged. "Where else?"

"You mean, he's with one of the squaws over at Tipi Town?"

"I ain't swearing to it, sir."

Matt tried hard not to smile. Windy Mandalian, the company's chief scout, was famous for his scouting among the women in Tipi Town, the transient Indian

9

camp out beyond the deadline to the northeast of the post. But he became instantly serious. "Shit, I sent Malone to get him."

"Then he'll get him, sir. Private Malone knows something of the whys and wherefores of Mr. Mandalian's social life, since he himself is always trying to share it."

Matt looked again at the sky. "Nearly sunup. If they're going to attack, that'll be it. We've got maybe ten, fifteen minutes. What I want to know is, is it a decoy bunch out there sent to lure our full strength so they can hit us with a main force from somewhere out of sight?"

"Or is that line around the post their entire force?" said Cohen, following Kincaid's line of questioning. "'Course, who knows how heavy it is?"

Matt turned now to look right at Cohen to emphasize his point. "In either case, the question is why are they waiting for full daylight when they could have attacked much more easily a half hour ago? Even without the sun in our eyes, we'd still have had trouble seeing them." Kincaid paused. Then he said, "Do you smell something, Sergeant Cohen?"

"A rat."

"A rat," said Kincaid. "Maybe Mr. Lo *wants* us to see him."

The first sergeant's voice was flecked with honest admiration as he said, "If I may say so, sir, you even think like an Indian."

"Maybe," Kincaid said. "Maybe. Maybe it's a habit you fall into out here." He grinned suddenly at the big, burly sergeant. "Doesn't matter, does it, just so long as we keep our hair on."

But his face was troubled as he looked again toward the east. Where the hell was Windy? Without another word, he turned and walked quickly toward officers' country.

Meanwhile, Ben Cohen, feeling a stab of pain in his

10

guts, cursed Mess Sergeant Dutch Rothausen again for the condition he was suffering. Although, at the same time, he was beginning to harbor the suspicion that just possibly the blame might be laid to the bottle of tarantula juice he had bought from Pop Evans, the sutler, the night before.

Captain Warner Conway, commanding officer of Easy Company, had vaguely caught the distant sound of Private Gribble's call for the sergeant of the guard. Struggling out of a sweet, deep sleep, he discovered that his wife, Flora, was lying right on top of him. Shifting his body as well as he could, for her elbow was jammed into his liver, the captain sought to extricate himself without waking her. But she moaned and murmured, and now, snuggling closer to him, began to resume the activity in which they had engaged upon going to bed only a few hours earlier. The captain could do no more than oblige his lady.

They had just consummated their action when there came a brisk knock at the door. With a muffled curse, the captain began removing himself from his wife's entwining arms and legs.

"Oh, Warner, do you have to?"

"Duty, my dear." And he called out, "Who is it?"

"Kincaid, sir. Sorry to disturb you, but there's an alert."

"Right with you, Lieutenant."

Minutes later, the commanding officer of Easy stood in his office while his adjutant and second-in-command handed him a cup of coffee and apprised him of the situation. Conway was a veteran of the frontier, in his middle forties, beginning to go gray at the temples and to expand a little at the waist, yet he was alert and vigorous—as Flora would readily agree.

"The men?"

11

"They're mostly posted, sir. A few minutes. And sir, it's almost sunup."

"Got it."

"I've called the platoon officers, Captain. We're awaiting your orders."

"It appears to me you have everything well in hand, Lieutenant."

"It doesn't look good, sir, but on the other hand I can't say it honestly looks bad," Matt said, and then told Conway of his wondering why the hostiles were waiting.

Captain Warner Conway studied what his adjutant had said. He knew Matt Kincaid was not given to superfluous speech and that he meant exactly what he said. In short, if it stumped Kincaid, then it'd stump anybody.

Carefully the captain reviewed the situation. "You're saying it could be some young bucks hankering for action, or it might be building up to a full-scale attack to wipe out the post. In the first instance, they're hoping for a skirmish so they can count a few coups; in the second, we're in big trouble."

"Sir, I figure that since they left their horses and moved in on foot, it could easily be a nuisance skirmish. Or a decoy."

"Holding back the main force for the rubout when we move out to hit this bunch." Warner Conway looked into his coffee cup. "Well, here we go again."

The two men were silent for a moment. Kincaid watched his CO. He had known Conway and served with him a long time. Each respected the other, and they were on a first-name basis on informal occasions. By all rights, Conway should long since have been promoted to major; Kincaid himself rated a captaincy. Both men were held back in grade because of the economic depression that had begun under the Grant administration, and from which the country was only now beginning to recover under the reforms instituted by the newly elected President Hayes.

Conway had served as a lieutenant colonel in the War, but had been reduced in rank at the end of that conflict, like hundreds of other officers. Sometimes Matt wondered if it was because Conway was a Virginian, even though he had fought for the Union. Conway himself had never put forward that view; after all, even Custer had been reduced from major general to captain!

Matt Kincaid had just missed the war. At the time that hostilities had ceased, he was a mere cadet at the Point. He'd graduated in '69, and this was his second Western tour of duty. Although he had been cited for bravery in action against the Comanche on the Staked Plains, the powers that be in the War Department had not yet seen fit to promote him to captain. Hence it was a common bond between the two men that they were overage in grade, and this was occasionally the subject of whiskey-tinged conversation at night in the headquarters office when things were quiet.

And things were often quiet on outpost duty on the High Plains. Easy Company was a unit of mounted infantry—dragoons—guarding the approach to the South Pass through the Rockies. Easy Company was also expected to maintain a strong military presence in the heart of Indian country. It wasn't an easy job, in spite of the company's appelation, with the small number of soldiers available; but as the saying went—and it was said again and again—"If it don't kill you, it'll make a man of you." Or, as some humorist put it, "We can still be the toughest soldiers in the graveyard."

"Don't believe I can add anything, Matt," Conway said. "I'll see the ladies are alerted. We'd better get cracking now." He scowled, and then said, "Hold morning muster and do everything as usual. And have the men

13

keep their weapons with them during breakfast. The main point is, Mr. Lo must not know we've spotted him."

"Yes, sir."

The two men went outside together, both looking immediately at the lightening sky.

"Hell," said Conway.

Walking into his quarters, Warner Conway found that his wife was fully awake. She was, in fact, partly dressed, sitting on the edge of their bed, brushing her long, almost jet black hair.

Conway stood just inside the door, admiring the stunning beauty who had married him. He could never figure out why she had, though she told him often enough—and showed him in no uncertain terms—that she loved him madly.

In her late thirties, Flora Conway was adored and respected by every man in Easy Company, a fact that made her husband justifiably proud. She was a surrogate mother to any young wives on the post, and to young men when necessary, listening to their problems and offering down-to-earth advice. It was no secret that she was a definite softening influence on the CO whenever it came to her pretty ears that, in his zeal, Warner Conway might have been overly harsh with a young recruit.

As for the other long-standing army wife of Easy Company, Ben Cohen's Maggie, she adored Flora Conway and would have done anything for her, claiming to her husband that "herself," as she called the commanding officer's lady, was lacking in only one department: that somehow the Good Lord had forgotten to make her Irish.

It was almost full daylight now when Kincaid walked into the mess hall. He told Dutch Rothausen the situation, telling him to order up hardtack and bully beef if the situation grew to a full-scale fight instead of a skirmish. The mess sergeant, a massive three-striper who also served as company medic, had been baking since the wee hours and was sweating profusely.

"Yessir." He nodded vigorously, spraying sweat in Kincaid's direction.

"And Sergeant, set up your litter bearers and medical post."

That's it, Matt told himself as he hurried out, throwing a glance at the stable. He had already told the handlers to have mounts ready for pursuit if needed.

Suddenly he felt the light stronger on him, and he turned to see the edge of the sun just at the horizon.

Still at his post on the east wall, but now backed by Sergeant Gus Olsen and First Platoon, Gribble had become more aware of the hostiles out beyond the deadline. For some while he'd not been able to see anything that he could really identify, though Olsen had pointed out a number of things. The nervous Gribble was glad that Sergeant Olsen, like Cohen, was willing to teach him.

"It's your life, and everyone else's," Olsen had put it to him. "So you'd better know what's going on."

It was still difficult to see, even though there wasn't much protective cover for the hostiles. The dim light, the dark color of the attackers, who blended with the tawny brown grass and earth around the post, made it hard to detect anything until it moved.

Gribble was itching to fire at something, at anything. He had gotten over his shock at discovering that the peace between the Indians and the whites was simply an illusion; and now he wouldn't have been able to say whether or not he was ready to face his first action. He was so keyed up that anything would be a relief.

"Try to loosen it," Olsen said, speaking suddenly, and Gribble jumped.

The sergeant had gone off to check his men, and now had come up behind him without a sound.

"I'm all right, Sarge."

"Sure you are. But I don't want you getting jumpy and shooting at something. You know the orders."

"Right, Sarge!"

Kincaid's orders: not even to aim at anything until the order was given.

Now he suddenly felt a strange silence fall on the outpost, and realized to his surprise that there wasn't even the sound of a bird; it was that moment immediately before dawn, when the sun prepared to sweep the sky.

Beside him, Olsen spoke. "Right on time. The lieutenant sure picked it, by God!" And the sergeant's words were lapped by the crack of a Springfield rifle.

Kincaid, hurrying across the parade toward the east wall, felt the sun on his hands and face. Throwing a quick glance in the direction of the stables, he saw that his order for available mounts was being carried out, and that Rothausen's detail had collected litters. On the other side of the parade he spotted a squad of men running, holding their Springfields at port arms, their Smith & Wesson handguns flopping at their waists, the holster flaps cut off for easy access.

"I want the reserve squad on this side," he shouted. "And on the west wall, you spread out more!"

Reaching the foot of the east wall now, he looked quickly to see if Lieutenant Carter was set up. He had placed the new second lieutenant where he could keep an eye on him, taking charge of the First Platoon himself, as he often did. The gate, in the east wall, was the weakest spot in the post.

"Will they use fire arrows, sir?" Carter asked as Kincaid appeared at his side.

"They might. Got your bucket brigade ready?"

"Yes, sir." Then Carter added eagerly, "Good thing it's all cleared around the post. The ground, sir."

Matt eyed him. He was used to green second lieutenants, it being his job to break them in. Yet there was

16

something about Carter that was different. A kind of urgency, an aggression that showed in his answering almost before the other person had finished speaking. He had a very red face, and he moved his hands a lot, indicating to Matt that he probably had a bad temper coupled with a strong tendency to criticize.

"The main thing, Lieutenant, is to watch for smoke," Kincaid said.

"Smoke?"

"They use it as a cover if they plan to ram the gate, probably with an uprooted telegraph pole. I'll be on that parapet, at least for the moment."

He reached Gus Olsen's side just as the first wave of hostiles came running across the hard-packed, dry ground.

The firing had accelerated on both sides. Now the first wave of horsemen drove down on the east wall, many of them firing Springfields, rocking from side to side on their mounts, making tough targets for the soldiers who had the added difficulty of the sun in their eyes. At the same time, arrows flew in at the defenders, though the range was still not close enough for accuracy.

Kincaid watched the wave of riders break and circle back as half the men on the parapet released a concerted salvo of fire and then swiftly reloaded while the other half fired.

"Looks like we can handle them, sir," said Carter, coming up in answer to Kincaid's signal.

"That'll be their first wave," Matt said thinly.

"But we turned them, sir." Carter's voice was insistent, with the strain of argument in it.

"They turned themselves. Mister," Matt said, hard, turning on him, "you got a few things to learn. See that line that moved in behind them on foot? Those are their marksmen. You didn't spot them while you were watching their cavalry and that first decoy line, did you?"

17

"No, sir. I have to admit I didn't."

Sergeant Olsen, inevitably chomping on a plug of tobacco, let fly a jet of brown juice, splattering it against the sod wall.

"That is for sure, Lieutenant; and I'm saying, sir, with all due respect, it takes a sharp eye to notice them devils infiltratin', and a cool head too, sir."

Olsen, stocky, tough as a McClellan saddle, had served in the War. He and Matt Kincaid had been together from the day of the latter's arrival at Outpost Number Nine. There wasn't an elisted man in the field whom Kincaid trusted more than Gus Olsen. And it was Olsen who, along with Kincaid, broke in the second lieutenants that Conway invariably assigned to First Platoon for "training," or as Ben Cohen put it, "for drying behind their ears."

"What guns are the hostiles firing, Mr. Carter?" Kincaid spoke without moving his eyes from the regrouping Sioux cavalry.

"Springfields, sir. Near as I can judge."

"Pinpoint that, Mr. Carter."

"Springfields, sir."

"And ours?"

"Also Springfields, sir." Carter showed his surprise at the question, and Matt could feel his annoyance.

"Then, Mr. Carter, what do you figure from that situation?"

"Equal firepower, sir?" Again, Carter tried not to look puzzled, but Matt read him easily. Carter was in his early twenties, and it was his first firefight. Fresh from West Point, he and his wife had been only shortly at the post, and Matt knew both of them were finding it difficult.

"Equal firepower," Matt repeated, "and you'll notice that they come only just inside the deadline."

"It's a rum one, that, Lieutenant, if I may say so," Olsen said, spitting again to emphasize what he saw in the strange behavior of the hostiles.

"You're saying it will be a standoff, sir?" Carter asked, still trying to catch Kincaid's drift.

"The question is why," Matt said.

Suddenly Olsen barked out, "Dobbs, keep that big punkin head of yours down, for Chrissakes!"

Private Stretch Dobbs, lean as a telegraph pole, hunched down behind the sod wall, just as a bullet thudded inches away from him.

"Looks like they're getting the range now," Carter said, speaking to no one in particular, but trying to retrieve some of his self-importance.

"That one already had its ride," Kincaid said. "The range is still too far."

"If only we had Spencers, sir."

"They got 'em," Windy Mandalian said, suddenly appearing behind them. "They got Spencers. I seen one of 'em."

"Then why don't they use them?" Carter asked, looking at Kincaid and ignoring the scout.

Windy didn't mind. He was used to upstart West Pointers. He said, "Because they got something else in mind, that's why."

"What would you say that is, Windy?" Matt asked. He had his eyes on the horsemen who were waiting behind the deadline, thinking maybe they would use the Spencers this time—knowing, too, that twenty men using firing repeaters could easily equal forty with Springfield breech-loaders.

Windy Mandalian scratched deep into his wiry beard and spat, almost hitting the same place Gus Olsen had targeted a moment earlier, then said, "Dunno. I only know what you know, Matt, and that is, you can never tell what them hostiles is up to, exceptin' for sure it's no good."

Matt squinted from beneath his campaign hat, one

hand on the butt of his Scoff, the other on his pearl-handled Colt, both at his belt with their butts forward for a cross draw. The Colt was his one indulgence in weaponry. It wasn't regulation, but as with the cut-off flaps on the Scoff holsters issued to the company, many COs in the frontier army wisely leaned toward efficency rather than spit and polish.

Kincaid let his gaze run over the rolling swells of purple and dull orange toward the east, and now turned to look south beyond the trampled dust of the fenced and empty horse paddock. Well, he reflected, they'd find out what Mr. Lo was up to in a minute or two.

Meanwhile, Lieutenants Fletcher and Williams, commanding Second and Third Platoon respectively, had taken over the west and north walls, leaving the east and south to Kincaid and Carter and First Platoon.

But the main action was at the east wall, only sporadic firing coming from the other directions.

"Lieutenant, they're not regrouping!" Olsen suddenly cried. "They're withdrawing. They're pulling back."

"Send a runner to check the north and west walls, Sergeant. It might be a feint."

"Yessir!"

It was true. The attackers were all the way behind the perimeter now, and there was almost no firing at the other walls. The fight had died to desultory bursts. Through his field glasses, Kincaid watched the Oglallas moving well out of range.

"Casualties, Mr. Carter?" Matt called out.

"None, sir. First Platoon all present or accounted for."

"Take a look at that, Matt!" It was Windy Mandalian, and his eyes were riveted to a spot off to Kincaid's left where a dozen hostiles were gathered.

The Sioux had been pulling back, widening their circle, except for this one place where about a dozen of them were collected on foot. Now, without warning, two men had broken away and were coming at a dead run toward the post gate. Instantly the Sioux began shooting at the pair, who were zigzagging to make themselves uncertain targets.

"Hold your fire!" Matt shouted to the men on the wall. "Cover them with fire to their rear!"

Slugs from the Indians were kicking up dust around the two runners, who were coming on fast. The pair were lucky. In another moment they were out of range.

All at once, three of the Sioux broke from the group and started after them, but at an order from Matt, the soldiers opened fire and drove them back.

Both sides now watched the two runners struggling on their last legs toward the gate. They were clearly spent, though obviously young and in good condition. Matt ordered the gate opened, and in another moment they were inside Outpost Number Nine.

"Sergeant Olsen."

"Yessir, Lieutenant."

"Go down and greet our guests. I'll be along directly."

"Yessir."

Even while speaking to Olsen, Kincaid had not taken his eyes from the departing Sioux. He continued to stand there watching them as they turned and moved off.

"Sir."

"Yes, Mr. Carter."

"The hostiles have withdrawn all around the post's perimeter, sir."

"Very well." Through the glasses he was watching one of the Sioux horsemen as he rode away. He wondered who it was as his eyes followed the rider until he was out of sight. He lowered the field glasses, still holding the vision of the rider, with his straight back and regal bearing, his grace of movement, and—obvious also—his pride.

"Well, sir, maybe we didn't kill any Indians," said

Carter, "but at least we caught ourselves two prisoners."

"Except, Mr. Carter," Kincaid answered slowly and with cold emphasis, "you might have noticed that those captives happen to be whites." And he added, "And very young ones at that."

two ━━━━━━━━━━━━

"Thank you, gentlemen, thank you." The commanding officer of Easy Company held the door of the orderly room for his departing platoon officers, meanwhile nodding to Matt Kincaid to remain.

Closing the door firmly, Conway released a long sigh and, looking over at First Sergeant Ben Cohen and Corporal Four Eyes Bradshaw at their respective desks, smiled wearily. Then he walked into his office with Matt following.

"Shut the door, Matt, and drag up a pew."

Matt chuckled as the captain moved behind his desk and lowered himself into the familiar swivel chair, reaching as he did so for the wooden cigar box. He opened it and selected a long, thin cigar with a dark wrapper. Then he pushed the box toward his adjutant on the other side of the desk. "Have one."

"Thank you, sir." Matt enjoyed Conway's cigars, which were infrequently offered; this was not because the captain was at all stingy, but because the two men seldom had time to relax. Nor was it that they were really relaxing now, but it was definitely a time for measured, careful exchange. Matt could see that his CO was just as puzzled as he was himself.

He watched Conway bite off the end of his cigar and spit the little bullet of tobacco in the general direction of a cuspidor—an item that looked as though it had been with the army as long as he had.

"It's fishy, Matt. There's something fishy about it." Conway had struck a match now and was leaning back in his swivel chair, the cigar between his fingers, the match burning in his other hand. Now he leaned forward and held the flame for Matt, then lighted his own. Meanwhile, Matt had been wondering if the flame, which was rapidly moving down the wood, was going to burn the captain's fingers. But Conway made it without mishap, and now, pushing way back in his chair, he drew on the cigar and released a thick, odorous cloud of blue smoke, which his eyes followed as it rose to the ceiling of his office.

"You feel they let them get away too easily; is that it, sir?"

Conway's eyebrows lifted. "Unless the Sioux are losing their eyesight, for God's sake. They could have dropped them a dozen times." He sighed. "I don't know. Sometimes I think this post is getting to me."

Matt considered the ash forming on the end of his own cigar. "Maybe they just didn't want them. You know, some of those white kids can be more trouble than they're worth."

"I know that," replied the captain ruefully. He was thinking of his nephew back in Richmond. "I know that."

"Do you think they let them escape on purpose, then?"

"I'll be damned if I know. Hell, if they wanted to get

24

rid of them, why didn't they just hand them over? Why all the circus?"

Matt was about to mention Windy Mandalian when there was a knock at the door.

"Come."

The scout, his long, bony body clad in buckskins, scowled and, following the indication of Conway, took a chair. He was carrying a cup of coffee.

Windy, tall, laconic, and often lugubrious, revealed all the insouciance of a professional civilian in the employ of the U.S. Army—especially the professional scout. Windy Mandalian, it was said, didn't take it from anybody; but as it was often pointed out by Matt, who was probably closer to him than any other white man, he didn't have to. Yet Windy, all the same, was never out of line. Like Kincaid, he was known as a straight-shooter. And like Matt, he was respected by the Indians.

Conway put his forearms down on his desk, leaning forward. "Let's get the straight of this now. You two have spoken with the kids. I want to hear."

Matt and Windy exchanged glances. Kincaid was struck, as always, by the likeness Windy bore to the Indians. He was Armenian on his father's side, but his mother was said to be the offspring of a French Canadian fur trader and a Cree woman. This was gossip, of course, since Windy was notoriously close-mouthed about his origins—as he was about everything else. Long, stringy black hair descended from beneath his wide, flop-brimmed hat, and his face was adorned by an unsheared growth of sparse black whiskers. His eyes were concealed, except in moments of surprise, by thick eyebrows. The central point of his resemblance to the Indians was his nose: an impressive, large-nostriled, beaklike affair of burnished dark red hue. Also, he *moved* like an Indian, and many said he thought like one—and he seemed to prefer their company to that of whites, with the sole exception of Matt Kincaid.

Matt was about to speak when Conway called out through the closed door, "Corporal Bradshaw, can you come in here with pencil and paper? I want you to take some notes." He turned to Matt and Windy. "Of course, Regiment will want a report."

Four Eyes Bradshaw always seemed slightly overwhelmed by his own glasses, and was always a little nervous, especially in the presence of Conway, Kincaid, or Ben Cohen. When the corporal entered the office, he saw that there was nowhere to sit, so he hurried back to his office for a chair. When he was finally settled, the captain turned again to Matt and Windy.

"The names," Matt said, "are Will and Walt. They claim to be twenty, but I judge it more like seventeen." He cut his eye at Windy, and the scout nodded in agreement.

"Still tender in the feet—though the Sioux did toughen 'em up some."

"Will and Walt," Conway said. "Last names?"

"Kenning."

Four Eyes looked up from his writing pad. "Which one is Kenning, sir? William or Walter?"

"Both," Matt said.

"They're brothers, then," said Conway. "I see."

"They are *twin* brothers," Windy said.

"Twins...that's a funny one." Captain Conway raised his eyebrows, his lips pursing.

"And they're as alike as two peas in a pod," Matt said.

Bradshaw's mouth fell open. "You mean, sir, you can't tell them apart?" He was suddenly covered with confusion. "Sorry, Lieutenant, I didn't mean to interrupt, sir."

His apology was ignored as Conway started to laugh.

He ended up coughing, wagging his head. "Lord, we get 'em, don't we? Identical twins. I suppose the Sioux figured they were magic or something, eh, Windy?"

"I got the notion the Sioux figured they were too damn much trouble," said the scout sardonically. "White kids are usually a heap big pain in the ass to them."

"They're from Georgia," Matt said. "Orphaned by the War, raised afterward by such relatives as they had left, sent from one place to another. Eventually they hooked up with a wagon train and went as far as St. Joe, then picked up another train heading for Oregon. They made it to Grease Creek, then the Sioux hit them. Everyone killed except Will and Walt."

There was a pause, and Matt looked down at the toe of his boot.

"So what else?" Conway asked. "They're getting fed. Looked to me like they needed clothes, though I only saw them far off. And we'll have to contact Regiment." He stopped, eyeing Kincaid and Mandalian. "What's up?"

Windy, sitting easy in his chair, shrugged casually. "That's *their* story," he said.

Conway sniffed. He looked at Matt, who simply wrinkled his forehead.

"When did all this happen?" Conway asked. "When did the Sioux take them?"

Matt looked at Windy. "I asked Will. He said last October."

"Walt told me they were took in January." Mandalian sniffed.

"Maybe the boys were shaken up some, you know," Conway said. "Got their memories scrambled or something."

"Sure," Windy said. "I also asked them how the Sioux treated them."

"And they said?"

27

"They said the food made 'em sick."

"They know what tribe?" Conway asked. "Are they Owl Feather's people?"

"Said they didn't know."

"How the hell could they not know?" barked Conway.

Matt said, "Neither one ever heard of Owl Feather."

"Goddammit," Conway said, sitting up straight in his chair, "I want to know how they were treated. Did the Sioux try any tricks on them?"

"They don't look or sound like there was any torture," Matt said.

"They did mention a couple of names—Bald Eagle, Crying Horse," Mandalian put in.

"You know them?"

Windy shook his head. "I got no notion. Could be anybody."

"What I want to know is why the Sioux attacked, or appeared to attack the post this morning. Did you ask them that?"

"They both said they didn't know," Matt replied. "They said they didn't even know there was going to be an attack; though they did know something was going on when they saw the warriors painting up."

Conway shook his head. "Maybe they just can't remember," he said, raising his cigar. "Poor kids." He drew on the cigar. "And they just decided to make a run for it? Just like that?" He shook his head again. "Well—maybe that's the way it is."

"They're funny," Mandalian said, his voice low; he let a long sigh run all the way through his long body. "Can't put my finger on it. 'Less, of course, they're scared, just plumb scared."

Warner Conway turned quickly on his chief scout. "It happens, we all know that." He looked at Bradshaw. "Corporal, you sent the message to Regiment?"

"Yessir."

"Their medic will know. Or maybe he will," he added, seeing the sour look on Windy's face.

"They act it," Matt said. "I mean, scared. They're just too quiet—holding it all in, or something."

"Funny," Windy said again.

"It happens with captives," Conway said. "It's one hell of a shock."

"No," Windy said. "I mean it's funny the hostiles didn't kill 'em when they wiped out the wagon train."

Conway grimaced and looked down at his hands, lying on the desk before him. Then he whipped his eyes toward Mandalian. "So what does that mean?"

"I dunno," he looked at Conway. "Then I asked 'em if they knew anyone named Two Coyotes or Fox."

"Those two renegades?"

"The very same," put in Matt.

"And what did they say to that?"

Matt sat forward in his chair as he said, "They both said they never heard of either one of them."

"So?"

"So this, Captain." Windy put his empty coffee cup on the desk. "I seen Fox this morning. I seen him as clear as I see you. Had the glasses right on him, settin' a little blaze-face black pony."

"Ah," said Matt, remembering the warrior he had noticed when the Sioux were drawing back.

There was a short silence, and Matt said, "For them to have been in the tribe since last fall, or even since January, and not know a couple of braggarts like Fox or Two Coyotes..." He let the rest of it hang.

Conway was nodding slowly, taking it in. "Hell, a whole lot of them speak English; it isn't like there was no communication at all." He lifted the cigar thoughtfully. "Yes, they'd have to know." And then he said, "Do you think Owl Feather was behind this?"

"I don't believe so," said Windy. "Hell, he wants

peace, but those young renegades are pretty feisty to handle. Maybe old Owl Feather just ain't chief anymore."

Matt was nodding along with the scout. "But a rascal like Fox would brace those kids for certain. They'd just have to know who he was. Only if Owl Feather can't hold the tribe together, our asses are in big trouble." He looked over at Windy. "Tell the captain what else you saw."

Windy had been carving a chew from his plug of tobacco with his bowie knife. Now he paused with the fresh chew and knife held in midair, his eyes on Conway. "Seen somethin' real interesting, Captain."

Warner Conway prided himself on being a patient man, though neither his wife nor Matt Kincaid would have wholly agreed. Their side of the question would have been quite evident now as Conway began drumming his fingers on his desk and biting his lower lip.

"Windy, will you either get that damn plug of tobacco into your mouth and chew on it, or leave it on that knife. But tell what the hell you saw!"

Matt had a lot of difficulty in keeping his face straight at that.

"I seen the weapon Fox was packing with him."

Windy popped the chew into his mouth, and now for an infuriating moment he chewed. Finally, with his cheek bulging, he said, "It just happened to be a Spencer."

Conway sat back in his chair, bolt upright. "Then why in hell didn't he use it? I didn't hear anything but Springfields. How do you figure that? Lack of ammo?"

"Could be he just didn't *want* to use it," Matt said. He looked at the scout, who, with his chew taking up all of his attention, was looking for the spittoon.

Quickly, Conway pointed, and bending, Windy let fly; his aim was reasonably accurate.

Conway turned now to his adjutant. "Matt, I want to

see those two kids. Tell Cohen to get them here." He
stood up, hitching at his trousers. "By God, we'll get to
the bottom of this."

"Captain's expecting us, Sergeant," Matt said as he
walked into the orderly room with Will and Walt Kenning.

"Come in," called Conway, whose door was partly
open.

Both Ben Cohen and Four Eyes Bradshaw were staring
openly at the former captives of the Sioux.

The captain, meanwhile, had swung open his door
and walked out into the orderly room. "Come in," he
said, and held out his hand. "I'm Warner Conway, commanding officer of Outpost Number Nine. Come on in
and sit." Conway turned, his sharp glance sweeping the
boys, noting the reluctance in their handshaking, the lack
of expression in their faces.

They followed him in, with Matt bringing up the rear.

"Sit down. Matt, will you close the door?"

Matt said, "They've eaten, Captain. And Sergeant
Cohen is securing quarters for them."

"You'll want rest," Conway said, sitting down in his
swivel chair. "And, uh, baths..." He sniffed, then covered it with a cough. He had never cared for the bear
grease the Indians rubbed on themselves, and the two
boys seemed to be loaded with it.

"Rothausen has the KPs boiling water, sir. And supply
is rustling up clothes," Matt said.

"Good."

They were all seated now, and the captain turned his
full gaze on the two Kennings.

"Which one of you is which?" he asked. "You're,
uh—Will, are you?"

"I'm Will."

"I'm Walt."

31

Matt grinned. "Harder to tell you fellows apart than the spots on a pinto horse."

Both nodded. They were thin, clearly underweight, yet by no means sickly.

They were good-looking boys, with brown hair, widely spaced eyes, also brown, and strong bodies. Both Matt and Conway studied them as covertly as they could, trying to find some way to tell them apart. But they were identical.

"I'll bet even your eyelashes are the same," Kincaid said suddenly.

"How old are you, boys?" said the captain.

"Twenty, sir," one of them said.

"I think we might put that at seventeen, eh boys?" said Matt with a friendly smile.

"That's a generous figure," Conway said. His voice was kind, but he was making it clear right off that he was taking no nonsense.

The boys looked at each other and said nothing.

"You've got Georgia accents, if I am not mistaken."

"That's right, Captain."

"What part of Georgia?"

"Near Atlanta, sir."

The other twin said, "Captain, you sound like you are from the South, sir."

"I'm a Virginian, young man. And I am now a captain serving in the army of the United States of America. I say that because I detect a certain, uh—question in your voice?"

Matt looked at his CO in surprise mixed with pleasure. He sometimes tended to forget how really sharp Warner Conway could be. At the same time he was glad to see the boys' responsiveness.

"Do you boys remember the War?" Kincaid asked. "I know you were pretty young then."

They were silent for a moment, regarding the captain

32

expressionlessly. Finally, one of them said quietly, "We remember it, sir."

The tone of the answer didn't seem to invite further inquiry; Conway threw a look at his adjutant and said nothing.

Matt looked closely at the pair again. Their faces were beardless, their cheeks smooth. Both had down on their upper lips. Their voices had turned, and they even *sounded* exactly alike. Their clothing was a mixture of store-bought and Indian. One of them—was it Walt?—was wearing high shoes, while Will wore Sioux moccasins.

"And so, how did you wind up way out here?" the captain was asking. "Would you mind telling it again? I know Lieutenant Kincaid and Windy Mandalian have already heard it, but..."

The boys looked at each other.

"Did you just run away?"

They were shaking their heads. Will bit his lip.

"Nope," Walt said. Then added, "No, sir."

Conway looked at them thoughtfully. "Maybe we can talk about it later," he said. "When you've had a chance to rest up."

Walt started to scratch his head, while his twin brother sniffed.

"I take it that there wasn't much left there to keep you in Georgia," Conway said gently. "That the way it was, boys?"

The two heads nodded. Matt watched Will—or was it Walt?—biting his lip. And then suddenly he realized it wasn't sorrow he was reading there in the two of them; it was anger.

Conway couldn't have been kinder. "I was through that part of the country," he was saying. "But after the war. I did my fighting up around Gettysburg, Antietam." He paused, then went on, "We'd better get this straight.

Lieutenant Kincaid here wasn't in the War, though a few of the enlisted men were. None of the officers, save myself. I want that straight in case there's hard feelings. But the War is over. I am still serving in the United States Army and I am proud of it."

The boys sat motionless in their chairs, their backs straight, their hands on their knees. Almost like they were in church, Matt thought—or maybe a courtroom. Yes, he thought—anger.

"I think that's enough for now," Conway said suddenly. "You'll stay on the post here until we get orders from Regiment. You'll have the freedom of the post— up to a point. Sergeant," he called out. And Matt felt the shock of Conway's instant return to army protocol.

When Ben Cohen entered, Conway said, "Get these young men settled, Sergeant. I've told them they have the freedom of the post. You'll indicate to them what that means."

"Yessir."

The boys rose, their eyes on the captain. Then, without a word, they turned toward Ben Cohen and followed him out of the office.

When the door had closed behind them Conway said, "Where's Windy?"

"Scouting up whatever he can get on this morning's little visit, sir. You remember he was going to take a swing west anyway to check on his tribes. I don't look for him to be gone too long."

"I hope he comes up with some answers." He paused, eyeing his second-in-command carefully. "You think I hit 'em too hard, Matt?"

"No, sir. I think you put it to them straight. That's the only way. They're snotty and they're still fighting the Civil War."

"They'd call it the War Between the States."

"They weren't giving a thing."

"They'll get over their anger—some day. But you can't blame them. Sherman didn't play tiddlywinks when he was down there, and neither by God did Grant."

Matt nodded. "I don't know what Reb doesn't hold some hard feelings for the Yanks, when you get under the surface half an inch."

"What do you think we ought to do with them? Regiment might push 'em off on us awhile. They're not always fast at coming up with solutions to problems."

"I've been thinking about that, sir." Matt rubbed his chin thoughtfully. "I'd suggest we have Ben give them some details. Be hospitable, but make them earn their keep. No nonsense, though they're still not army; but keep them busy and meanwhile we'll watch them." He added, "I guess you can see I don't feel too easy about them either. They just don't seem shaken much by their visit with the Sioux."

"I'm glad we see alike on this, Matt. Right now I want to know what the Sioux are up to. and how these kids fit in—if they do."

"Sir, with your permission, when Windy gets back, I'll be riding out with First Platoon to try to locate Owl Feather and see just what the hell's going on. I somehow don't feel he was behind this morning's action. But he always seems to know what's up."

"You took the words right out of my mouth," Conway said, grinning. "Either there's a treaty or there isn't."

three _____

That spring the snow had stayed late in the land. It had been a hard winter, and now life had begun slowly to return. Now the land softened as the creeks and rivers filled with the melting snow. Fresh color had started in the trees, and the grass stretched over the prairie. Now, as its growth built momentum, spring time filled the earth more swiftly.

This day the jays and chickadees called, while the great sky felt the sweep of eagle and hawk. Those buffalo that were left had dropped their coats, and in the tall timber and long valleys the wild game moved with fresh vigor over the awakening earth.

In the cool forenoon, the long line of the wagon train lay across the floor of the valley like a lazy whip. Horses and wagons moved slowly, sinking into the soft earth, leaving behind the deep wounds of their passage.

High up on the rimrock that defined the edges of the valley, Windy Mandalian sat his horse. He was not watching the wagons that were advancing slowly toward the West; he was studying a clump of pine, not very far from where he was. Only a moment earlier a jay had risen from the little trees, calling.

His dark eyes now went to the wagon train, yet he still held some attention on the clump of pine. For though he was looking at that scene far below, he was still aware of the immediate territory around him. It was as though he were listening—only listening not just with his ears. He was listening the way he had been taught by the red man, and by his years. He was listening with the whole of his body, the whole of himself, aware of the sounds, the smells, the movement of life there. Like the Indian, Windy Mandalian knew the life of the earth, the timber, the rocks. And it was to this he listened.

They are coming like sand, he was thinking, and they will cover the earth. Nothing will stop them. The Sioux cannot stop them. It was as Owl Feather had predicted. Owl Feather had dreamed it and had told it to him. Owl Feather, the son of Riding Eagle.

Windy kneed his blue roan, shifting his weight, and now began to pick his way down the trail toward the wagon train. It took a while.

The long, probing line had stopped, and he knew that he had been seen. Now as he reached the floor of the valley, three riders rode out to meet him. They came at a gallop on not the best of horseflesh, Mandalian noted, while he walked the roan toward them.

The man in the middle, the biggest of the three, drew rein first and his companions followed suit. They had pushed their horses over the sludgy ground, so Windy knew their inexperience, and knew also their feelings toward many other things. Greed, he was thinking; it caused a lot of grief.

Windy Mandalian had big hands, the bones visible in outline beneath the skin, and he kept them close to his weapons—the bowie knife, the big blue Navy Colt, the breech-loading Springfield—as the big man spoke.

"Howdy, mister." The tone was affable, though careful. "Know if there be water up ahead?"

Windy took a moment to size the man before answering. He could hear the impatience in the words, and the other's need to be first, to be the leader.

"There's water yonder," Windy said. "Past that butte, then to the creek. Your horses know it."

He watched their surprise, and then the big man said, "Too bad they didn't tell us. Well—dumb animals..." And the three of them laughed abruptly.

Windy said, "And there's a band of Sioux up ahead too."

His words brought a swift exchange of glances among the three.

"You mean—you don't mean hostiles?"

Windy spat over the roan's withers and said, "Depends on how you treat 'em. 'Course, you happen to be on their land."

"Their land?"

"This is the country that was given to them in the treaty they signed with the U.S. Government. You're trespassing."

"But the army is here to protect us!" It was the man to Windy's left—a man with no hat, no teeth, and maybe no hair too, Windy thought, for he had a blue bandanna tied tightly around his head.

"The army's here to keep the peace, which means neither the Sioux nor the whites break the law. You men are breakin' the law."

"Bullshit," said the man. Then he caught the look on the scout's face, and covering himself, he asked, "How many would you say, mister?"

"Enough to bury your wagon train."

The third man spoke to that. He was a tight, bony,

and somber-eyed man, in his fifties, Windy reckoned, and he figured him for a preacher. He had that stiff-spined look, and he lived high in his shoulders and chest, his clothes tight on his body. "We were told that this region had been cleared for whites to pass through, or settle."

Windy said, "They'll likely hit you by nightfall. I'd judge it the other side of that stand of timber." He nodded in the direction of where they could expect the attack. "My advice is to haul out of here, and right now. I mean, if you want to think of your women and children." He paused and his eyes went past them to the wagons. "If you got any."

A short silence held the four of them, and then the man Windy had taken for a preacher said, "But do they have rifles? Repeaters? We have Spencers. How many can they be that we can't give them a sound whipping!"

"Mister, it is your business."

"I mean, we can't just be run off by a bunch of savages. People want to come West, build homes, settle the country."

Mandalian spat over his pony's forequarters. "It is not my business," he said again. And he took up his reins.

The big man in the middle said quickly, "We appreciate your words, mister. Name's Tobler. This here is Frank Miller and Preacher Johnson."

"No hard feelings," Tobler said suddenly.

Windy Mandalian nodded.

As they prepared to turn their horses to ride back to the wagon train, Preacher Johnson said, "Didn't catch your name, mister."

"That's right," Windy said. "You didn't." And he turned the roan and started back the way he had come.

Later, from a stand of spruce up near the rimrock, he watched the Sioux wipe them out. It took a while, because, as the preacher had said, they had Spencers. But the Sioux were too numerous, and whoever was leading them that day had his medicine working for him.

When there was nothing left but a few wisps of smoke from the charred wagons, when the very last of the defenders of their land had departed, Windy rode down.

It was not the first time he had borne witness to such a scene, yet he still felt that pull deep in his belly and legs as he looked upon the remains of those who shortly before had been living beings.

Carefully, for he wanted to be sure none of the attackers returned, he dismounted and examined the remains of the wagon train. After he had left the three men some hours earlier, a suspicion had been growing in his mind. When he saw the charred remains of a wooden crate, he knew he'd been close to right. The attackers had left no Spencers, but what remained of the crate told what the white men had been carrying as at least part of their load; and anyway, what he couldn't see he could smell.

Windy Mandalian looked at the sky, then down at the scattered, mutilated bodies. "Goddammit," he said, though the words came out more as prayer than imprecation.

He had ground-hitched the roan, and now he gathered the reins in his left hand, grabbed a handful of mane, stepped into the stirrup of his battered stock saddle, and swung up and over.

The sun was moving swiftly down the long sky as Windy Mandalian rode swiftly for Outpost Nine.

A dog barked, and now another spring morning touched the dark plain, feeling over the sod walls of Outpost Nine, and on to officers' country and the enlisted men's barracks, the sutler's store, the empty paddock, and the stables from which came the sound of horses stamping and an occasional low nicker as the hostler approached with grain.

As the light quickened, subtle colors touched the softening land. Lance Corporal Reb McBride bugled reveille, and the post stirred, the men of Easy Company slipping with grumbling ease from sleep to the routine of duty. It was another day, a day of drill-and-wait, of work details and rumor and boredom—a day like yesterday, the day before, the day before that...

Only this was not to be a day like all the others. It was McBride who spotted the rider pounding in past the perimeter, the dry ground booming like a drum under the streaking horse. By the time Windy Mandalian and the blue roan reached the gate, it was already open to let him in.

"Whiskey!" Conway bit the word as he sat facing Windy and Matt Kincaid in his office.

"And Fox and Two Coyotes on the prod." Windy shook his long head dolefully. "It'll be a first-class shit storm."

"The question," said Matt, watching Windy thoughtfully, "is who was it bound for?"

"Maybe it was only one, two crates," Mandalian said. "Hard to tell. Those men didn't 'pear to know where they was heading. New to the country. Then they might've been figuring to sell it theirselves. Or..." He spread his hands, shrugging the shoulders of his buckskin shirt, wrinkling his face. "Or could be it was for their own use." He sniffed. "Which I doubt."

"Thing is, was it maybe a whole operation to sell whiskey to the tribes?" said Matt.

"Best way I know to rile up Mr. Lo and stir trouble," Conway observed. "With the heroic army quelling the uprising."

"Amen," intoned Kincaid.

42

"And meanwhile the whites have moved in." Windy's words were punctuated by an enormous expectoration of tobacco juice, almost swamping Conway's spittoon.

The captain looked at the scout in astonishment.

"What about Spencers?" Matt asked.

"Fox and Two Coyotes get 'em now," Windy replied.

"Do you think they've got a bunch of them?" Conway asked. "Spencers? I mean, you saw one with Fox out on the perimeter here. Then there are those from the wagon train. Could there be more?"

The scout nodded. "More'n likely." He reached into his shirt and withdrew a plug of tobacco and now began slicing off a fresh chew with his bowie knife, as he leaned forward with his elbows on his knees. "Mind you, he wasn't showing that Spencer off. I only just caught a glance at it. So it could be he didn't 'specially want us to know." Lifting the blade and tobacco chunk to his mouth, he accepted it eagerly in his jaws and immediately began chewing. "On the other hand, he might've," he concluded, his words mumbling past his chew. "Huh! Spencers and whiskey. They nose their way to the bottom of all that scamper juice, they'll really have to go to sign language."

Conway, watching him in covert amazement, wondered how the scout could handle such a chew at one time. Dropping his eyes to the cuspidor at the side of his desk, he sighed inwardly with the realization that shortly it would be splattered with another load of brown spittle.

Sure enough, the scout suddenly let fly, splattering that receptacle with matchless accuracy. Conway would have felt badly if he'd missed.

"Sir, I think we'd better talk to Owl Feather," Matt was saying. "We've got to find out fast where he stands."

Conway was nodding vigorously even before he finished. "I agree with that. What do you think, a platoon?"

"Should do it, sir. We don't want Fox and Two Coyotes hitting the post while we're out."

"And they might just be looking for that," Conway added.

Windy seemed to unwind his long frame in the chair in which he was coiled, laughter coughing out of him as he spoke. "You got them two hotshot kids to whipsaw things here. What d'you need soldiers for, huh?"

A grin spread out over Matt's face. And Conway said, "Boy, when I meet kids like those two, I thank God I'm not a father." He paused. "I also have to remember that murder is illegal."

Windy boomed out a laugh at that.

"Windy, you don't know the half of it," Matt said.

"They've moved in, have they?"

"They have, shall we say, gotten over their initial inability to communicate," Conway said wryly.

"I seen what they was when they first come in," the scout maintained. "They don't listen to nobody and they think their asses is solid gold." He looked questioningly at the two officers, one eyelid lowered in a sly wink. "What have the little darlin's been up to?"

"What haven't they been up to?" Matt said. "They've been up to everything except hard work; and I believe our kindly first sergeant is about to explode."

"The wages of sin and bein' civilian," said Windy.

"I assigned Sergeant Olsen to keep an eye on them," Matt said, shaking his head sadly.

"And what?"

"Those two monsters took him into town and got him into a poker game where he lost everything, and they got him as drunk as a snake on Indian River whiskey."

"No shit!" Windy's eyes were dancing.

"That's only one episode in the two days they've been here," Conway added. "One of 'em got into an argument with Private Holzer, calling him a dirty German or something like that. The other one—who the hell knows

44

which is which?—braced Malone. Jesus! What the hell did he say?" He turned to Kincaid.

"He called him pigshit Irish," Matt said. And then to Mandalian, "But it was Malone and Holzer ended up fighting each other. The kids didn't lift a hand!"

"You can see why Fox and Two Coyotes could've been glad to be shed of 'em," Windy said sardonically.

Serious again, Conway said, "I think First Platoon, Matt. It'll give our new lieutenant a chance to work off some of his piss and vinegar."

"And it will keep Malone, Holzer, and Sergeant Olsen away from our sweet little orphans."

"I think Sergeant Cohen will have to step in," Conway said.

"And myself on the patrol, sir? I want to talk to Owl Feather."

"Of course. Yourself and our faithful, honorable, and durable scout here." The captain was smiling as he put his arm on Windy's shoulder.

When they walked out of his office and into the orderly room, Conway looked over at the first sergeant, seated gloomily at his desk.

"Nothing from Regiment, Sergeant Cohen?"

"Nothing, sir. They're still thinking on it, I guess."

"I'll send another message if we don't get something today," Conway said.

Matt paused at the door. "How are our young guests, Ben?"

"The little dears are still asleep. I just hope that nasty old reveille bugle didn't disturb them, sir."

"Maybe Regiment is smarter than we give them credit for," said Matt with a laugh.

"Cohen caught them running a dice game in the barracks last night," Conway said to Mandalian.

"Too bad I wasn't around," the scout answered blandly.

"You know we overlook a *little* cardplaying and dicing now and again," Matt explained. "On the post, that is."

"Good for the soul," Windy said. "Let me know when there's a game."

"If I might say something . . ." Ben Cohen began. The first sergeant's tone, Matt noted, was heavy with patience.

"Fire away." Windy had paused, his hand resting on the edge of the door, which he had just opened.

The glowering look on Cohen's face had changed to one of wicked humor. There was a glint in his eyes as he said, *"If"* — and he was heavy on the word — *"If* there is ever another dice game on this post while them two sweethearts are here, I will be pleased to let you know."

Windy picked it up fast, to Conway's vast appreciation. "You mean," said the scout, "they don't lose."

"The bastards cleaned up." Cohen wagged his big head. "Hell, if it ain't the one, then it's the other. And oh! all sweet and innocent-like!"

Windy was already shaking with laughter. As he started out the door, he looked back at Sergeant Cohen. "Hell, the Sioux's loss is our loss. You could put it that way. Yeah—I think so." And he went out, shaking his head.

Conway watched his top kick mutter something. His face was straight now as he said, "Sergeant, I am turning these two young men over to your personal care. I have full confidence in your ability to handle the situation in your usual exemplary manner—which will, of course, conform to all military regulations."

"Yessir," Cohen said briskly, and snapped a salute at the captain and the lieutenant as they went out.

When the officers and Windy had been gone for a moment, Four Eyes Bradshaw looked over at Cohen and said, "Sarge, can I ask you something?"

"You've already interrupted my thinking, Corporal

Bradshaw, so you might as well continue."

Flushing, Four Eyes held his ground. "Sarge, why do Indians like to gamble so much? I mean, everybody says that about them."

Ben Cohen put down the pencil he had been playing with. His chair creaked as he leaned back in it. "Why does anybody like to gamble?" he said. He reflected a moment, and then continued. "Hell, it's fun. And it beats hard work."

Four Eyes was staring at the sergeant. "Sarge, why do some people never lose? I mean, why are they so lucky?"

"I dunno, Corporal. Maybe those kids are just too dumb to lose."

"Pardon me for saying so, but they don't seem dumb at all to me."

"That's what I mean, Corporal. They're too dumb to be smart. See, so they don't outsmart themselves," he added as a look of dismay filled Bradshaw's face. And he shook himself at the thought of the twins taking nearly a whole squad of Second Platoon for their month's pay.

four ─────────────

Edwina Carter, young, pretty, and proud to be the wife of a handsome young officer in the United States Army, looked around her quarters in crumbling dismay. Over everything lay a film of fine yellow dust. Even now, as the soldiers tromped back and forth on the parapet overhead, more dust floated down from the ceiling. She looked at the hard dirt floor and at the two rugs she had brought from back home, which were now permeated with dust. Picking up a cloth, she crossed the room to the wall mirror and wiped away the film that made it impossible to see any reflection.

She stood there looking at her face in the mirror, noting the lines at her mouth, the wan expression of the blue eyes, the straggle of the thick blond hair. She felt itchy, dirty. And suddenly a tear rolled out of her right eye and started down her pale cheek. Then, without warning, her body began to shake and she was sobbing uncontrollably. Throwing herself on the settee, she buried her face in her hands, no longer making any effort to contain herself.

At first she didn't hear the knocking at the door, and when she finally became aware of it, she wanted to call out to whoever it was to go away. But the knocking persisted, and at last she rose and, dabbing at her eyes with her handkerchief, called out.

"It's Maggie Cohen, my dear," came the voice from the other side of the door. "Can I chat with you a minute?"

Edwina was seized with panic at the thought of the first sergeant's wife seeing her in her present condition. Had she heard her sobbing, she wondered. Now she looked at herself again in the mirror and almost burst into tears once more. Her face was red, her eyes puffed from crying; she looked and felt in total disarray. Only there was nothing for it but to let her visitor in.

"I'm sorry," she said, opening the door at last, the tears again in her eyes, but not actually flowing. "I am feeling rather poorly. Maybe it's the vapors. Please come in, if you can bear to let your eyes fall on me, Mrs. Cohen."

"Don't give it a thought, Mrs. Carter," said Maggie, coming in and closing the door behind her. "And will you call me Maggie, my dear."

"And I am Edwina, please."

For a moment the two women stood looking at each other: Maggie Cohen, plump but still very well proportioned, a dark-haired, blue-eyed woman with an ample and firm bosom; and Edwina, a good deal younger, lithe and lissome in comparison, not quite frail, and yet with a firm jaw, although now it was again beginning to quiver. And in another moment she was in Maggie's arms, her body shaking again with sorrow and anger.

"Come, come, sit down," Maggie urged, drawing her toward the settee. "Now then, my dear, just let it all out. Crying's good for a body, washes out the pipes. I do it myself. It's like an occasional drop of booze, good for what ails you."

Maggie's lively blue eyes looked around the room, noting the dust, which was still falling from the ceiling as someone tromped along the parapet above.

"It's murder for sure," she said. "But that's the way of it. Better the dust than bullets and arrows, I always say. I've the same problem in my own house, with the feet traveling back and forth whenever there's an action, like now with the drill. And my man, Ben—would you believe it?—he doesn't mind. Only when the dust gets into his supper."

Edwina had straightened up now and was drying her eyes.

"Cold water on the face," Maggie said, rising and stepping swiftly into the next room for a pan.

Returning in a moment with a pan of water and a cloth, she said, "Wash your face, love; I'll help you get started cleaning up the mess. But first maybe we'll set a spell."

Suddenly Edwina burst out, "Oh, I'm so unhappy! I hate it here. I hate it!"

"There, there, love, you'll get over that. You know, it's one of the best outfits in the army, so I've been told. And I believe it."

Edwina stared at her aghast. "I'm so lonely. And this . . . this . . ." She held out her hand, looking at all the dust. "And Dennis, I hardly see him at all. And I'm not certain this is the place for him, either."

"Your husband's with the best man he could be with," Maggie said stoutly. "Matt Kincaid. He'll teach him the ropes better and quicker than any man alive. They'll be back in a day or two."

"It's that Dennis wants so badly to fight the Indians. You know, that's all he's been talking about, ever since we came. It's really gotten . . . well, he talks about it all

51

the time. Maybe this patrol he's on will work some of that out of him. I don't know."

"What's he got against them?" Maggie asked.

"He just keeps saying how awful they are and how they deserve to be completely wiped out."

"Could be he simply wants to ride out and fight like a man—you know, be a soldier and all that. He'll work it off soon enough and settle down, and so will you. A man gets restless, setting around the post doing nothing." Maggie winked. "'Course, with a good-looking lady like yourself, he'd be a damn fool to be doing nothing. Sorry, Mrs. Carter—Edwina—I don't mean to get so personal."

"You see, you see," said Edwina, looking down at her hands, which were folded in her lap, "Dennis has never been under fire. Oh, he's not afraid. Quite the contrary. He can't wait for an engagement with them. It's just that—well, I'm afraid Dennis is headstrong. He sometimes charges in without thinking. He . . . he has a frightful temper, Mrs.—Maggie. And sometimes I get frightened thinking what if he lost his temper in some battle or something and did the wrong thing?"

Maggie Cohen gave it thought. She had an idea of what the young Lieutenant Dennis Carter was like. She had known someone like that once, not too long ago— a headstrong, arrogant, dashing officer who had almost created a disaster but had been ultimately saved by Kincaid's guiding hand. She remembered Matt talking about it to her husband, remembered his saying that the man was trying to be another Custer.

Maggie Cohen was not one to dwell on thoughts, but this did come to her mind as she listened to Edwina Carter talking about her husband. She decided she would bring it up with Ben, who could pass it on to Lieutenant Kincaid if he saw fit.

Now she said, "A lot of men are like that. They want action. You know, it's like yourself, you get bored setting

52

around here with little to do, don't you?"

Edwina nodded, suddenly feeling better.

"Well then, my dear. It's the same with him. He signed on to be a soldier, and he wants to act like a soldier, not like some drummer peddling clothes and hardware."

Edwina suddenly discovered herself smiling now as she looked at the warm, open face of her companion. "Your husband is a lucky man, Maggie," she said.

"Ah! If he only had the sense to know it!"

The two of them had a good laugh at that.

Presently Maggie said, "I've come along with an invitation over to Flora's for a cup of tea. So why don't you get yourself together and we'll be off."

Edwina's face fell. "Oh, but I can't visit. I'm all covered with dust, and my clothes are—"

"Now look, I'll tell the mess sergeant to have the KPs fix a tub of good hot water for you; but meanwhile, it's time to get over there. You look all right. You know, we all have the dust, and we all have husbands, and we all have all the rest of it." She paused, her blue eyes laughing, her hands on her wide hips, her chin high. "You just need to brush your hair a little, if I may say so."

When Captain Warner Conway walked into his quarters later that afternoon, he found his wife having tea with Edwina Carter and Maggie Cohen.

Flora beamed at him with pleasure. "Oh, Warner, how good of you to show up just now. We were talking about the two young men who were rescued from the Indians. How are they?"

Conway gave a little shrug, wishing his wife hadn't brought up the subject, and said, "They're all right. They've obviously been through an ordeal, but they're young and resilient. They'll be just fine. Excuse me, ladies." And he started into the other room.

"Dear, do sit down and have a cup of tea with us," insisted Flora, turning one of her fondest smiles on him.

Conway could feel himself melt under her adoring gaze. Yet he didn't want to sit around with three women. At the same time, he did want to get to know Edwina Carter a little better. It was the first opportunity really to see her without her husband. To himself he had almost added the words, *without the restriction of her husband*. Yes, Carter was an inhibiting factor there, he could see.

"Thank you, my dear," he said, and sat down, smiling at Maggie Cohen, who grinned back at him.

"Will the young boys be needin' some maternal care in the way of mended socks and such, Captain Conway?"

Conway chuckled. "Ah, I do believe our noble first sergeant can attend to that very well, Mrs. Cohen. More than likely he's right now sewing on some of their buttons, the poor little fellers."

The whole group laughed at the picture of Ben Cohen sewing buttons, or anything else for that matter.

"How long will they be with us, dear?" Flora asked.

"That is entirely up to Regiment. And we've had no reply as yet."

"Because they might indeed require some things that only a woman can get for them—such as sewing."

"Could be. Could be," Conway chuckled, accepting the cup of tea Flora had poured for him. "You could have them to tea; is that what you're getting at?"

"Why not?" said Flora, and she looked at Edwina and Maggie, who nodded in support.

"We'll have to see about that, my dear."

There was a slight pause, and then Maggie said, "Captain, is there anything wrong—about those two?"

"Yes," said Flora. "You sound strange about them, Warner. They're all right, aren't they?"

"Oh, yes, I'm sure they're all right. It's just that until

54

we know a little more about them, we must go carefully. Just a word of caution, that's all."

He caught Edwina Carter looking at him now. "Captain, were they tortured by the Indians at all?"

"Oh, I don't think so. They certainly haven't said anything like that, and I think they would have if it had been the case."

"What on earth made you think of that, Edwina?" Flora asked.

"Just something Dennis said to me."

"What was that?" Conway asked quickly.

A slight flush mounted to Edwina's cheeks, as she felt herself caught out somehow.

"Just something my husband said," Edwina repeated. "He said that the redskins were savages who tortured the whites at any opportunity."

"That's not quite the case," Conway said shortly.

"Well," said Flora, quickly steering in another direction, "I'm sure if anything like that *had* happened, they would have said so. And as long as you think they're hale and hearty, dear, then there's no worry." And she smiled at her husband.

"Matt Kincaid is out locating Owl Feather to see what he can dig up about the attack this morning; as you know, your husband's with him," Conway said, looking at Edwina Carter. "He couldn't be with two better men than Kincaid and Windy Mandalian for learning about the ways of the Indian."

"I'm glad to hear that," Edwina replied. "Thank you, Captain Conway."

"And meanwhile," Conway continued, "the boys will work on the post here. It will keep them occupied and will pay their way. It can also benefit us in certain areas where we're shorthanded."

"That sounds like something right up my husband's alley," Maggie said. "I swear, that Ben Cohen can find more things for a man to do than you can point your finger at."

Everyone laughed at that.

"And that's just one of the reasons he's a real top sergeant," Conway said, putting down his empty teacup. "More, Warner?"

"No, thank you, my dear. I must get back. Just wanted to check in for a minute." He stood up now and, bending toward her, kissed her lightly on her high forehead.

When the captain had departed, the three women poured more tea. Flora could see that Edwina Carter had something on her mind. While she had been preparing the tea earlier, Maggie Cohen had swiftly filled her in on the scene in the Carter quarters when she had listened to Edwina. For a while the girl had seemed to have, or possibly recovered from her doldrums, but now she appeared to be upset again.

Flora, being Flora, took the bull by the horns.

"Edwina, I feel you have something on your mind, dear. What is it? Is there something I can do?"

Edwina looked down at her teacup, which she was holding with both her hands. She shook her head. "Thank you. Thank you, but I don't think so."

She felt Maggie's eyes on her, but she still refused to look up. And then, as she heard Flora clear her throat lightly, she spoke. "I guess there is something on my mind."

"What is it, dear?" Flora leaned forward, her voice soft as she studied the younger woman.

"It's ... it's ..." And then she looked up to meet the eyes of both women. "I want Dennis to put in for a transfer."

"But my dear, you just got here." Flora sat back in her chair, putting down her cup and saucer.

"I know. But I ... I ..." She turned her tortured gaze full on Flora Conway. "I like you, I like all of you. Really I do. But I hate it *here*. I hate it!"

56

． ． ．

In the hot forenoon, Matt, Windy, and the First Platoon of Easy Company picked their way along the iron-hard trail. They had ridden up close to the rimrock, and now were descending to where sagebrush gave way to buffalo grass. The morning was tranquil, and for a moment Kincaid felt lulled by a serenity he had not known for some time. A jay suddenly calling reminded him with a shock of the need for constant vigilance.

Windy and Conway had both agreed with him about taking the whole platoon, in case the hostiles decided to visit any of the settlers, or possibly set up an ambush; and also the men needed the action. Boredom was always one of the most dangerous aspects of life at an army post, for a man could grow slack and, as a result, could become instantly dead. Yet the main purpose of the patrol was to contact Owl Feather. Both Matt and Windy were pretty certain that the attack on Outpost Number Nine had not been mounted by the whole tribe of which Owl Feather was considered chief—at least by the whites. Rather, it was the work of Fox and Two Coyotes, who were impatient with the older ones of the tribe who felt that their best interests lay in getting along with the whites. They considered any accommodation of the whites a sign of weakness, even cowardice.

Matt took the time to explain it to Carter, for he could see how eager the green lieutenant was to lock horns with the hostiles.

They had just crossed a rocky, shallow creek and were starting up a long draw, and Carter was feeling the altitude. Kincaid had noted how pale he was, and had cautioned him. But Carter was not one to give in easily to physical weakness.

"Wouldn't it make good sense, sir, simply to capture Owl Feather and keep him until the Indians knuckle under?"

"It wouldn't do much good, Mr. Carter, for a number of reasons. First, Owl Feather is not the only chief of the Oglallas. In the tribes, chiefs are elected, not simply born to it. And they are elected according to the issue at hand. There's no such thing as a permanent chief— something the whites still don't understand, even though we elect our own chiefs. And second, Owl Feather is peaceful. He's no problem. It isn't him causing the trouble."

"Sir, with all respect, I feel a strong hand would save a lot of trouble in the long run."

"You mean a strong hand like, uh...Custer?"

"I was actually thinking of Captain Fetterman, sir."

"Yes—the Wagon Box Fight is clear in all our memories," Kincaid answered dryly.

"But sir, if I may say so—Captain Fetterman had a view of the redskins that seems to me to hit the nail right on the head."

Matt tried hard to keep the weariness from showing in his voice. He had had all he wanted of these spunky West Pointers who thought they had the world by the balls and just had to charge in and the tribes would fold at the sight of them. He watched Carter's brow wrinkle as he marshaled his argument, praying that he wouldn't feel it necessary actually to quote Fetterman's boast. He'd heard it all before. But he was not spared.

"'Give me eighty men and I would ride through the whole Sioux nation.'" Carter sententiously intoned what had become Fetterman's valedictory, and Kincaid winced. Did these greenhorns never learn?

"Nice words," Matt said. "But they did nothing to keep his whole command from being wiped out, Mr. Carter. I believe you've got something to learn about the Sioux, and all Indians."

"I know there are things I don't know about them, sir, but I still—"

"The first thing you'd better learn, mister, is to respect them," said Matt, cutting in hard. And he wheeled his mount and cantered back to the rear of the column. He could feel his face and the back of his neck flaming in anger.

The platoon was strung out now, with Malone, the wild Irishman, riding point a good five hundred yards ahead, and Stretch Dobbs trailing far to the rear as getaway rider. MacArthur and Armstrong rode flank.

"Figure if Owl Feather's got any sense—which he has," said Windy, riding up to Kincaid, "he'll be watching for us. I mean, figurin' he didn't have anything to do with that little action at the post. He'll be worried. 'Course, if he did, then it's a different story."

"But he will have heard about it in any case."

"Indians hear about everything," Windy said.

"I would think he might be around Willow Creek."

Mandalian spat over his horse's withers as he turned his gaze on Matt.

"Best spot for maneuvering, it seems to me, Windy." Matt squinted at the high sun.

The scout nodded approval.

Windy Mandalian's lined face remained totally without expression "You know Owl Feather," he said finally. "He is old, and that's for sure. But he sure isn't silent with the Oglallas. Sure, Fox and Two Coyotes make a big noise, and the young bucks get taken by that, but we all know Owl Feather don't want any splitting off. He knows he can't beat the whites, so he's trying to get that across, telling them they can't whip us and drive us out—there's too damn many of us—so they better learn to live with us."

"Thing is, how much say has he still got?" Matt put in. "A few fancy raids by Fox's band—coups, scalps, and all that—and those young braves won't listen to Owl Feather."

Mandalian said nothing, but just spat again.

The white sun was straight overhead now as, in the thrumming stillness of the heated day, they rode over the lip of a draw and down into a big, lush meadow. Matt listened to the jangle of rifles in their saddle spiders, the squeak of leather, the thump of horses' hooves on the fresh ground.

He had sent more scouts out—two Delawares, working under Windy—and now, receiving the all-clear, began crossing the wide meadow. When they had almost reached the other side, at a signal from the scouts he ordered the column to halt; the men drew rein to allow their mounts to feed on the rich bunch grass. Meanwhile the soldiers softened a little in their harsh McClellan saddles, taking their feet out of the stirrups or sitting swing-hipped and easy for a few moments.

"Well," Malone said, wiping sweat from his wide brow. "It'll be just as hot for them Oglallas as for us, by God."

"*They* don't wear clothes, for Chrissakes!" somebody said.

"Where are we heading, anyways?"

"Up shit creek, more than likely."

Olsen rode up to Private Haynes, a farmboy from Minnesota, with a shining thatch of albino hair. "What you got—the bellyache?"

The young soldier's face was the color of his hair as he shifted painfully in his saddle.

"Sure, it's a ball-breaker," Olsen said; and the men nearby gave out desultory laughter. It was an ancient joke.

"No . . . no, it ain't that, Sarge. I got the piles."

"Sweet mother of Jesus! I'm glad I'm not in your trousers, young feller." And the sergeant rode off, followed by a weak round of laughter, while Haynes sank further into dismay.

But in a moment Olsen was back, handing a blanket to the sufferer. "It might help, if you're careful. At least it'll be softer than that there McClellan."

"Thanks, Sarge."

Olsen looked at him sorrowfully. "Shit," he said, wagging his head in sympathy.

"Too painful, Sarge," Haynes replied with a weak smile. But this time the humor drew a good laugh from his buddies.

Dennis Carter rode swiftly up to Kincaid and Windy, who were sitting their mounts a little distance away from the platoon.

"Sir, I know for a fact that there is a hostile on our left flank, and he has been following us for some time."

"Thank you, Mr. Carter," Matt said. "You saw him over there, near that stand of box elders?"

"Then you've seen him, Lieutenant!"

Kincaid suddenly drew his rifle from its spider and, holding it above his head, waved it in a half-circle. Instantly an Indian on horseback appeared out of the box elders and repeated the signal. "He is Joseph Hatchet, Mr. Carter. One of our Delaware scouts working with Windy here."

Dennis Carter's face had turned scarlet. "Yes, sir."

Matt grinned. "Don't let it get you down, Carter. It isn't easy to learn it out here. The Point didn't teach any of us how it really is. You're not alone."

Carter looked even younger than his years as he let his eyes fall in embarrassment.

"But you better find your way to learning, because, like it or not, mister, those warriors know a lot more than you do. A hell of a lot more."

"Yes, sir."

They were silent for several moments. Then Carter raised his head and looked at the meadow.

"Sir, it's a beautiful country!" The words suddenly

broke out in spite of himself, and he was again flushed with embarrassment.

Kincaid laughed, suddenly liking the young man for his humanness. "It is the most beautiful country anywhere—I'd bet on that," he said. "Now you know one of the reasons Mr. Lo fights us so hard for it."

Matt watched the old Carter sweep back into the other's face even before he finished speaking.

"Sir, they're savages. They burn, kill, and rape. I fully agree with General Sheridan that the only good Indian is a dead Indian."

"Good?" said Windy Mandalian, suddenly looking at Carter. "What's 'good' got to do with it? You get an arrow in your guts, young feller, it won't matter what kind of hostile it's from—there won't be no good or bad about it!" And in disgust he stepped back into his stirrups and stood up. Still standing, he trotted his horse up to the clump of box elders.

"You learn to listen, Mr. Carter," Matt said. "I'm telling you again. I mean, unless you really want to become a permanent resident of this big, beautiful country."

Raising his arm, Kincaid signaled that the rest period was over. Quickly the column reformed and began to push through the mouth of the trail that led out of the meadow.

They had been riding about twenty minutes when Windy came riding fast down the trail.

"See that rimrock up there?" he said to Kincaid.

Matt nodded.

"Now let your eye drop just below." He pointed.

Matt said, "Got it."

"Hatchet just reported Oglalla up ahead. A lot of 'em, and all gussied up for war."

"How close did he get?"

"Close enough to smell the bear grease. He counted

thirty, but could be more. Says some have got Spencers."

"Then they must know we're looking for Owl Feather and they're figuring to hit us first."

"Looks to be the size of it," Windy said. "I figger Owl Feather and the main band are holed up in Star Basin. That's the other side of the big ridge down the valley, by Willow Creek."

"You think we can slip around Fox?"

Windy was shaking his head even as Matt was speaking. And before he could say anything, a shot rang out up at the head of the column.

"No," he said, with a tense smile. "I don't think we can slip around Fox."

Matt Kincaid had already kneed his horse and was barking orders.

five ─────────────

There were five players at the table in the sutler's back room—besides Will and Walt Kenning. So far the action had been slow. The dealer was Private Henry Parks, a short, stringy man with a lined face, very pale skin, and very quick fingers. He was one of Dutch Rothausen's kitchen team, and like the other cooks, he worked twenty-four hours on and twenty-four hours off. Parks was an inveterate cardplayer, and by the time his twenty-four "off" came, he was usually eager for action.

Picking up the deck of cards, he removed the joker and announced, "This is straight draw."

"Jacks or better," said Will, looking at his brother. "Good enough, I say." And the boys grinned at each other.

Besides the twins and Henry Parks, the game included four privates from Easy Company. The room, used principally for storage, was at the same time sufficiently out of the way for such activities as gambling or drinking, neither of which was encouraged at Outpost Number Nine, and in fact, in certain cases where the action went too far, were dealt with punitively. But boredom will drive even a good man to almost anything.

Parks dealt quickly, his long, thin fingers flicking at the cards. Will opened the pot for a quarter on a pair of kings. He was sitting to the dealer's right. Parks raised him twenty cents. Will stayed and drew three cards.

Parks's poker face turned into a wicked smile. He cleared his throat and said, "I play these."

Will said nothing, only emitting a sad little sigh. Parks glanced at the boy's small stack of money, calculating how much he had left.

Parks bet fifty cents. Will appeared to hesitate. It was in fact a long moment while the boy seemed to be struggling with his decision.

"I call," he said at last, and spread his hand, faceup, showing the two kings.

Parks could not conceal a look of utter disbelief. "I'll be dragooned!" he declared and threw his hand facedown in the discards. "Didn't you know I stood pat?" His pale face was twisted in disgust. "How can you call a pat hand on two kings?"

Will Kenning's face was the very model of youthful innocence as he looked at the older man. "Gee, I didn't know that," he said. "I'm pretty new to the game."

But there was a murmur of excitement now among the little group watching.

A few hands of stud were played, and now Ed Jones, private, third squad, Second Platoon, had the deal.

"We'll play draw," he announced, picking up the deck and again removing the joker.

Will and Walt passed. The next three players passed, making five in all. The sixth player, Big Tom Thompson of Second Platoon, opened with a ten-cent bet. Jones came out with a twenty-cent raise. Walt Kenning called, and drew one card.

"Gonna win it, are ya?" Jones said with a pleasant smile.

Walt didn't answer. Big Tom Thompson took three cards.

Ed Jones said, "I play these," meaning he was standing pat.

Big Tom, after a quick look at his cards, checked.

Without a moment's hesitation, Jones bet fifty cents. Walt hesitantly raised him a dollar, and a low whistle went around the table.

Thompson showed his openers, two kings, and folded.

Ed Jones shook his head sadly. "You lucky polecat," he said, and threw in his hand. "Imagine drawing one card with all that money at stake."

Walt tossed his hand in the discards and drew in the pot quickly.

"I guess it's just beginner's luck," his brother said.

This time the game was again stud. And the boys continued to win. Will took a hand, then Walt, and a soldier named Jed Barker took the third. The next round went to Ed Jones, who beamed with pleasure as he scooped his winnings into his campaign hat. "Ed Jones thanks you kindly," he said.

On the next hand, Big Tom Thompson squinted at his hand, whistled, and opened.

"You're bluffin', Tom boy," said Parks with a laugh. "I know you."

Then everyone dropped out except for the twins, Jones, and Thompson. On the next round, Will folded his hand.

Thompson drew one card and bet.

"Raise you," Walt said, advancing his money.

"And I up you," Big Tom said.

The betting shuffled back and forth among Walt, Big Tom, and Jones until there was a handsome pot in the center of the table—clearly the game's big hand. Big Tom was sweating into the red bandanna that hung loosely at his throat. Henry Parks, watching now, was humming to himself as he lighted a cheroot and looked over at Will Kenning, who had a simple little smile on his young face.

Walt leaned slightly forward. "I call, gentlemen. What have you got?" And Will shot him a glance.

Big Tom let out a coarse laugh and fanned his cards dramatically. Three tens stared up at the poker players.

"Not too bad," said Ed Jones. "But not good enough. Here, have a look-see: three fat queens, the way I likes 'em, an' a pair of fours. Yah!"

He leaned forward, his eyes gleaming at the pot. No one seemed to notice that Walt was still holding his cards.

Jones started to move as though ready to rake in the sizeable winnings, and just at that moment, Walt Kenning laid down his hand, showing four deuces.

"Glory be!" said Parks, his thin body quivering in awe.

It was just at this point that Sergeant Ben Cohen walked in. "So this is where you are!" he roared. "I might've known. Debauchin' the young! Jones, Thompson, the rest of you—I'll 'tend to you later. For now, by God, I want to see you two bucks in my office." He glared around the room, looking like a buffalo at whom some hunter had had the temerity to fire an arrow or bullet.

"Clear this place out now! All of it! You're lucky I let you get away with your assholes!"

And he swept them out of the room.

Crossing the parade, swearing to himself, Ben Cohen suddenly found himself thinking of Matt Kincaid.

At the precise moment that Ben Cohen's thoughts had turned toward him, Lieutenant Matt Kincaid was chewing out Lieutenant Dennis Carter for having discharged his rifle in opposition to orders not to fire, or even aim at anything, except under emergency circumstances. Unfortunately the lieutenant's bay horse had spooked at something along the side of the trail and somehow his rifle had gotten released from its spider and fallen. The bay had stepped on it and in a freak accident the weapon had discharged. Kincaid was furious.

Windy Mandalian, riding up to him, had grinned. "Easy, Matt. We need you cool, not all hot and hurried."

Kincaid grinned back at him, but tautly. "I know that. Only that damn fool might just as well have written the Sioux a letter."

"Mr. Lo has just dropped in," Windy said, pointing to tracks leading off to the right of the trail, in the direction of a stand of pine and spruce.

"Deploy the men in a skirmish line, Sergeant Olsen," Matt ordered. "Dismount!"

At the order, three men out of four dismounted, the fourth holding the horses and now moving them to the rear of the platoon.

Suddenly from the timber appeared a wave of Indians, riding toward the dismounted men of Easy Company, firing as they bore in close.

"Don't sound like they got too many Spencers," Windy said, after he had knocked a Sioux off his pony with his Springfield.

Kincaid, realizing that the Sioux were closing in on the left flank, which was not well protected, instantly ordered the line wheeled.

"That's the river over there on their other flank," Windy shouted above the firing. "There's high ground the other side."

Kincaid had already realized the situation, and now ordered his men to mount and charge through the Indian cordon to reach the higher ground on the other side of the river.

But owing to the dense dust kicked up by the Indian

69

ponies, as their riders raced back and forth, as well as to the smoke and general confusion, Matt reached the bank of the river only to find that a number of men hadn't seen their companions leave, and were left behind. The horse-holders who had remained back when the skirmish line was formed were having great difficulty holding the now-frightened animals. One or two of the horses even escaped and began running. In any event, these men were unhorsed and were forced to take to the brush to escape the withering Sioux fire.

Kincaid wheeled his mount, shouting to Mandalian to ford the river with the men who had reached the bank.

"Where is Mr. Carter?" Matt called to Olsen, who was directing his men into the water.

"Back with the rest of the horses, sir."

Kincaid swore. "Get up on that bluff!" he shouted to Olsen.

The sergeant repeated the order to the men.

Through the smoke Matt saw Carter afoot, facing two Oglalla warriors who were advancing on him. He was trying to fire his Springfield, but evidently it had jammed.

Olsen called something to Kincaid, but his words were drowned in the river as his horse moved slowly across; the whole platoon was under fire now from the warriors along the bank. Two men were hit, one screaming as he dropped his rifle and brought his hands to his neck, reeling in his saddle. Olsen, nearby, reached out, grabbing him by the arm. Together they made it across.

Matt had dismounted for better maneuverability and was running back toward Carter and the two Oglallas, firing his Scoff as he went. One warrior fell, the other turned and fired at Kincaid, who felt the bullet graze his left shoulder, causing his hand to open spasmodically, dropping the Scoff. Instantly his right hand swept in a cross-draw to the Colt, and he had the weapon up and out just as Carter charged at the warrior and brought him to the ground in a flying tackle.

Kincaid swore. He'd had the Sioux dead in his sights, and now he couldn't fire for fear of hitting Carter. Damn his heroics! The two men were grappling on the ground. The Oglalla was on his back, and Carter's hands were on his throat, strangling him. Matt saw the glint of sun on the knife blade. The Colt kicked once in his hand and the knife fell, the hand of the Indian smashed into a bloody pulp. Another shot and the Oglalla was dead.

Carter froze, staring down at the body he was straddling.

He looked up at Kincaid, his face scarlet. "Sir, I had him dead right there!"

"Mr. Carter, he had *you*." Matt looked quickly around. "We've got to move!" And when Carter, furious at being robbed of his kill, remained on the body of the Sioux, glaring at his superior officer, Matt exploded. "Mr. Carter, get your fucking ass moving!"

Turning, Kincaid plunged into the brush near the stand of spruce and pine. In a moment, Carter crawled in beside him. And none too soon, for all at once pounding hooves thundered by their hiding place as a half-dozen warriors swept across the dusty clearing, looking for stragglers.

At a sound to their rear, both Kincaid and Carter spun, their guns ready, but it was Malone and McBride.

"Any others get cut off?" Kincaid asked.

"No, sir," said Malone. "Only us—me and McBride."

"You were with the horses."

"Yessir."

"Sir, you're hurt," Carter said.

"Not bad. Just a crease." Matt had taken out his bandanna and was shoving it under his shirt.

Now, at the sound of firing from across the river,

71

Matt said, "Mr. Carter, we'll make a run for it. You lead with Malone. McBride and I will cover."

But now horses pounded again into the clearing, and the riders drew rein just a few feet away from Kincaid and the others.

They were lying in what must once have been a buffalo wallow in the sand not far from the river. Some thick brush growing around the hole pretty well concealed it from view. The Ogallas were still talking in the clearing just in front of their position, not more than fifty or sixty feet away.

"On your stomachs," Kincaid ordered. "Don't fire unless they see us. Mr. Carter, you face south; Malone, east; and you, McBride, face west. I've got north covered."

"Are we completely cut off, sir?" Carter whispered.

"We are. But it sounds like they've made it to the top of that bluff."

"That it does, sir," Malone said. "God bless 'em."

McBride said nothing. He had just thrown up, and was fearful the others might notice. But no one gave any indication.

"We're plumb smack in the middle of the bastards," Malone observed.

"It's all my fault, sir," whispered Carter, "my gun discharging like that—"

"For Christ's sake, Mr. Carter, things are tough all over." Matt almost snarled the words.

Malone hid his grin, while Reb McBride felt instantly better.

Kincaid sneaked a look at the sky, trying to figure how much longer the light would last. It was about the middle of the afternoon, which meant a long wait. If only the platoon could hold the top of the bluff and drive off the whole band. The only trouble was, the Sioux would probably draw back, and it would be to this point

72

where they were hiding. So it was only a matter of time before they were discovered.

Now there was movement in front of their position. Two warriors on foot had come quite close to where they were lying. But they had only come to pick up their dead and wounded.

An hour passed, then two, then three, and still they remained. Matt could feel his thirst rising and knew the others must be feeling the same; only it was too great a risk to move toward the river. His arm ached from the bullet crease, but he had Malone wrap it and he was able to move it well enough. Finally darkness began to obscure the clearing in front of them. The firing across the river had virtually stopped, with only a few sporadic shots now and then.

"We'll make a break for it in a minute or two," Matt said. "It'll be all right, even with the moon. Mr. Carter, you and Private Malone pair up. Stick together. I'll be with McBride."

Now the moon was up, and while they stood and looked about carefully, listening, they could neither hear nor see anything. The moon was shining through a haze, and it was not very bright. But Matt knew it would be suicide to stay in their present position until daybreak, with the Sioux very likely drawn back even now.

They had advanced not more than halfway toward the river when Kincaid suddenly froze. Only a few yards in front of him, a horse and rider loomed. As he stopped dead in his own footsteps, he felt the others freeze right behind him. The rider was cutting across at a right angle. just ahead of him, and he was followed by a second horseman, then a third. It was, he realized, a column of mounted hostiles. He remained absolutely still, trying not even to breathe.

After the column had passed, he let himself relax slowly; then, reaching back to McBride, who was directly behind him, he touched his arm.

Quickening their pace, but stepping even more cautiously than before, they soon reached the river at a point close to where the platoon had jumped their horses into the stream in their rush to gain the prominence on the other side.

"We won't try right here," he whispered to the others. "It'll be covered by Mr. Lo."

They moved on, and presently Kincaid stopped again, scanning the opposite bank for some trace of the spot where the others had climbed the precipitous bluff. He could discern nothing but a black, steep bank, towering high into the dark sky. A short distance to his right he made out a level piece of flat riverbottom.

Moving right up beside McBride now, Matt said, "I'm going into the water to see how deep it is. I want you to hold me."

Holding to some bushes at the edge of the bank, and with McBride gripping his shirt, Kincaid slid into the river. On the first plunge he went in nearly up to his neck, the current so swift it almost swept him off his feet. Quickly he climbed out, with McBride's assistance.

"It's too deep." He paused, listening. "But we can drink at least." They did, the sweet water bringing them needed strength. Quickly he washed his shoulder, with McBride helping; the water cooled and soothed the wound, which had stopped bleeding.

But the night was slipping away, and quickly Kincaid began exploring the bank of the swift-running river for a ford. Because the melting snows in the mountains at that season of the year sent all streams in the territory almost out of their banks, a crossing looked like a hazardous undertaking.

Now they continued their march slowly upriver, cautiously trying without luck to find a fording spot.

But finally a place appeared right in front of them that

looked as though it might be possible. Kincaid waded in and found the current less swift, the water reaching but a little above his knees. The others followed, and now they crossed to the far bank. Reaching the other side, Carter asked Matt where he thought the platoon was.

"I hope they're up on that bluff."

Suddenly shots rang out to their right.

"Quick!" Matt plunged into a bullberry thicket, with the others right on his heels. He wasn't sure if the firing had been intended for them, but he knew it was sensible to get moving anyway. Visibility was slightly better now, and they could make out their surroundings. The terrain was fairly open, dotted with thick clumps of bullberry bushes, some of them covering as much as twenty square yards. There were also some young cottonwood trees, and some tall, rank grass reaching to their waists.

When the moon moved behind a cloud, Matt signaled to them to cross the clearing, and he led the way swiftly to a clump of small cottonwoods, reaching it just as the hazy moon reappeared.

They had run across the open area spaced well apart, to avoid any cluster shooting in the event that the Sioux might spot them. But no shots had come.

Now, moving deeper into the timber, Carter again asked where the platoon might be.

"Across the river," Matt said.

"I don't understand, sir. I thought we'd already crossed the river."

"We did, Mr. Carter. Only we crossed to an island."

It was just at this point that they heard from one of the thickets nearby a startled voice hailing them. There was no mistaking the deep, guttural tones of the Sioux language.

six _____

By the pine tree on the hilltop, in the whisper before the dawn, surrounded by the last snow, the lone figure sat. Not a muscle, not an eyelash moved—only the sacred rhythm of breathing that was the same as that of the earth and the great sky above.

This was in the Moon of the Grass Appearing and it was the third day and he had neither eaten nor taken more than the proper sips of water. He had smoked, offering the pipe to the Above and the Below and the Four Directions. He sat facing west, for that was where the spirits were.

It was the third day, and now he listened to the chickadee, to the winged beings, and to the talking wind, the beings in and on the earth—the stones and the earth itself.

Now, all at once the bird-beings were silent, for it was the moment just before the sun came.

He felt the sun just as the winged creatures began

again to sing their songs. And he filled the pipe and offered it. He was an old man, though still vigorous. And he sat there listening to his prayer speaking inside him.

He continued to sit in the place that had been scooped out of the ground when he and Broken Horn had come; Broken Horn had helped him to prepare for his vision-crying. Together they had first built the sweat lodge and he had sat in it, doing everything according to instruction, slowly and well and in the sacred way.

Then, Broken Horn who was an Inipi medicine man, that is, one who could heal as well as predict, came with him to this high place. He, who was known to everyone as Owl Feather, and whom the whites knew as chief of his tribe, now lamented for his vision. For though this was his third day, he had not dreamed. Yet he would remain until the dream came to him.

It was cold and now there were strange beings all around him, and weariness and sleep pulled at him. But seated on pebbles, and with pebbles between his toes, he had stayed awake. Now, crying for his vision he sat.

The Thunder Beings came then, and a great winged creature with spots and long talons; and the winged cloud appeared and the Thunder Beings began to fall out of the sky. Soon the land was covered with them; and the sun came out strong and very red and the whole land was turned into luminous green grass. Then the winged creature with spots and long talons spoke.

When Broken Horn returned that day, Owl Feather offered him the pipe and told him what he had dreamed.

"The great winged creature told that many, many whites will come to our land. More than now, and that they will remain."

Broken Horn nodded.

Owl Feather said, "I know that it is so, for they fell into the earth and the grass grew very full."

78

"It is so," Broken Horn said.

"But the great creature also told me that the young men must be held in check. The two who attacked the bluelegs and then the wagon train by the Painted Butte."

"Fox and Two Coyotes."

Owl Feather nodded. "They have called the young ones, and now the Americans will think it is the whole tribe who are to blame."

"What is to be done?" Broken Horn asked.

Owl Feather raised his head to the lightening sky. "The white soldiers are coming to fight us. The being told me—as before when I dreamed—that we must not fight. They are too many."

Broken Horn nodded. "But for the foolishness of the young ones..."

"That was to be expected, since we are kept in one or two places and are no longer free. Still, we must hold the tribe together, or the whites will kill us all."

The old chief pondered a long time, smoking slowly, his eyes turned inward, while the new morning sunlight washed across the speckled land.

"It is so," Owl Feather said. And he emptied the pipe and cleaned it and put it in its sacred carrying sheath lined with rabbit fur.

He stood up, a tall man, straight as an arrow, clean in movement. Broken Horn waited to see how this old man who had fasted for three days and nights in the cold, wearing only a breechclout and a single blanket, would stand. Owl Feather stood strong, and his walk was steady as they descended to the village.

When they reached the village they heard news of the attack on Outpost Number Nine and the burning of the wagon train.

Owl Feather's heart was heavy as he turned to the older men who sat with him now in council. "And where are Fox and Two Coyotes and the young warriors now?"

"On the far side of Stinking Creek. The Americans are already looking for them."

Owl Feather said, "We must send a runner to the soldier Kincaid and the tall one who rides with him. A runner who will travel fast and not be seen."

"We must move camp," said an old warrior named Bull Climbs Up. "The soldier men can catch us here and we will be rubbed out."

"We must stay," Owl Feather said. "We have done nothing that is against the white paper. If we run, then we will be seen as having done wrong."

A murmur passed through the group sitting with him. But his wish prevailed. Shortly a runner was sent with messages for Matt Kincaid and Windy Mandalian.

"We must stay together," Owl Feather said. "We must keep ourselves together."

It was quiet in the enlisted men's barracks. The large room was almost deserted, save for Will and Walt Kenning, who were sitting on their adjacent bunks, facing each other. Ben Cohen had quartered them here rather than in the guest barracks, the better to keep an eye on them.

"Try it again," Walt was saying, and he watched his twin brother shuffle the deck of cards. "I think I'll catch it this time."

The boys were holding a large square board on their knees, making a table for their game, or as they called it, their "practice."

Will's hands moved like lightning as he dealt the hand for each of them. "Now then," he said, "I have got a hole card not showing, and an ace that is showing. Right?"

His brother nodded.

"And my hole card is also an ace." Will turned the ace faceup to show Walt. "And you have got a king showing and a king in the hole. We both have two other cards, because this is five-card draw, making it four cards each. Shit, do you really want me to go through the whole fucking preamble again?"

"Go on, go on," his brother insisted.

Will sighed. "You're right." He cleared his throat. "The point is, I have got aces over kings, and there's one card coming to each of us. So the betting's juicy."

"Shit take it," said Walt. "With these pikers! A quarter, ten cents. Hell, we haven't seen a decent-size pot since we gaffed Two Coyotes and Fox and their crazy bunch."

His brother grinned. "Who do you figure like gambling more—reds or whites?"

"Shit, the Injuns'll bet on anything."

"So will anybody, long's he's got the good odds."

Walt took the cigar out of his mouth, and spitting on the floor, he stared down at the globule of spittle.

"You don't want the sergeant finding that there, do you?" said Will.

His brother grinned and rubbed the spittle dry with the toe of his boot. "Fuck him" he said. "The Yank bastard!"

"Maybe that's the best offer the son of a bitch'll get all day," said Will.

"So all right," said Walt. "The floor will now pass inspection, Mr. Master Sergeant, sir!"

The boys chuckled at that. Now Will loosened his shoulders, holding the grimy pack of cards in front of him. "So, I am dealing, but I deliberately hold the deck in such a way that you can't help but see your last card will be another king." He demonstrated. "That means two kings showing and a king in the hole, which, in a real game, I would know was there. So you will have three kings to beat my aces. Right?"

"Right!"

Will grinned. "You see that king all right?"

"Sure do." Walt suddenly blew a cloud of smoke right into his brother's face.

"Cut that shit out!" snapped Will, coughing. "So watch it now. We bet. I have raised you, and you cover. By jingo, we've got a couple of thousand in that pot!"

"And your ass is made of solid gold, for Chrissake. Around this piss-poor dump, we'll be lucky to get a pot halfway up to your ass." Walt blew his next cloud of smoke toward the ceiling.

"I say we have got a couple of thousand—at least—in that pot! Now watch very, very carefully." Will's eyes were slitted as, with a little twitch of his left hand, he flipped a queen over his brother's cards.

"I saw a king!"

"Yes, dear brother. I am aware of that, yes indeed." And setting the deck down with his left hand, Will said, "Now I will take a card from the top of the deck." And with his right hand he took for himself the king, just where it had been all along.

Walt grinned all over his face. "Not bad. By God, not bad at all."

"You caught it?"

He shook his head. "Can't say I did."

Will picked up the cards. "Not bad, eh?"

"For a beginner," his brother added with a grin.

Throwing down the cards, Will shoved the makeshift table aside and threw himself at his twin.

In a moment they were rolling across the bed, landing with a crash on the floor, their arms and legs locked as each tried to pin the other's shoulders to the floor in a wrestling fall. Breaking away, they both stood again.

Walt had a reverse headlock on his brother and was about to throw him when Will suddenly went limp and stepped hard on his brother's instep. Walt grunted with pain, his hold slackened, and Will lifted him onto his shoulders for a spin.

It was just at that point that a bellow resounded from the doorway of the barracks. Dropping his brother, Will turned to see what it was.

It was Sergeant Ben Cohen, and his face was the color of fire. "What the hell d'you think you're doin' in this here barracks!"

Walt had gotten to his feet now, and both boys stood facing what could only be called the equivalent of a raging buffalo bull.

"You think you'll pull your goddamn shit and shenanigans on this post, do you! By Christ, there'll be none of that shit in my command. Now get your asses into a fast haul and clean this here up and by God report to me in my office! You've got ten minutes to be there!"

And he stormed out, livid with fury and decision.

"I have had enough of those damn kids," he told Corporal Bradshaw when he stormed into the orderly room.

"I think most of us have, Sarge." Four Eyes Bradshaw looked glumly at the first sergeant. Like Malone, Olsen, and not a few others, he too had suffered crushing defeat at the gaming table.

"Tell me, Corporal Bradshaw—do you think those two are rigging their games?"

"If they are, Sarge, they're damn clever at it."

"I am watching the clock," Cohen said, and his jaw was as hard as a rifle stock. "By Jesus, those two better have their asses in here to the minute!"

Meanwhile, back at the barracks, the boys were cleaning up. Nothing had been broken in their melee. It was mostly a matter of smoothing the beds, picking up two overturned chairs, and of course, collecting the deck of cards.

"Why don't we just tell Cohen to go fuck himself?" Will said. "We ain't in the army."

"But we depend on the army," his brother said sagely.

"I guess you're right."

"Cohen could make life real difficult for us, my lad."

"All right. But I don't like being threatened."

"Listen, this is an *out*post. Get it—*out!* That means the rules are lax, for the ones who run the outfit. That means a Cohen can get away with acting like king of the dungheap. He is one tough son of a bitch, and I for one would not wish to tangle with him as I have heard tell he is apt to do with any enlisted man who might see things different than himself."

"You mean you're scared of him."

Walt studied it a moment and then said, "Yeah, that's right. I was scared of Fox and Two Coyotes and I'm scared of Cohen. Nothing wrong with being scared, you dummy—at least you live to talk about it."

"Shit," Will said. But there was agreement in the way he said it. "Shit," he said again as they walked out of the barracks. Walt was right again.

"We have *got* to go along with him," Walt said as they crossed the parade. "I mean, survival is the only thing. So, all right, we'll do just what he says, we'll use him, and we'll behave nice so we can get what we want, which is to get the hell out of here—out of this glorious, beautiful, and magnificent goddamn West—and get back to civilization."

A grim smile started across Will's face. "Brother, I am reading it right along with you."

seven _____

Lance Corporal Reb McBride always said that had he known what he would be getting into when he joined the army, he would have gone muleskinning with his uncle Lije instead.

Reb, a bare twenty-two, sandy-haired and with a grin all over his face, was from Texas, and by golly everybody in Easy Company knew it. Reb, too young for the Civil War, was still a stout defender of the Lost Cause, albeit with much humor. He took a lot of barracks ribbing, but he gave it back too. His goodwill was unquenchable. But mostly Reb thanked whoever it was necessary to thank for the fact that he had ended up in Easy Company with Matt Kincaid.

At first he'd been a touch leery of the Connecticut Yankee West Pointer, and especially that hard, yet supple body and the bristling demand for discipline from which Kincaid never deviated. But he soon caught on to the fact that while Easy Company's second-in-command was cut-and-dried military, he could generate considerable humor in those blue eyes of his.

Reb had wanted the cavalry, but had been willing enough to settle for the mounted infantry. Still, he was not so sure he'd gotten what he wanted at all when he was put bareback on an animal built out of muscle, flame, and anger and set to jumping ditches and wood fences. Especially with that crazy sergeant bellowing at him to grip with his knees.

Reb had ridden mules and farm horses down home, and they'd sure been a whole lot more comfortable than those fiery army remounts. But worse was to come when he was ordered to saddle up and found himself atop a McClellan saddle with only one hope before him: to get off the damn thing with his balls still in working order.

Right now, standing in the tall grass on the island in the middle of the river, with the challenge of that hostile ringing in his ears, Reb found he was about ten yards away from the lieutenant. He saw Kincaid drop down in the tall grass, and in a split second he was hidden himself. He now heard a great commotion as six horses burst into the clearing where the four of them were hidden, and raced toward the river.

"They must've got themselves separated from their main body, too," Kincaid said, standing up. "We'd better move, in case they decide to come back with some friends." He sniffed. "Or they could have been pickets, in which case there are more nearby. We'll go real easy-like."

Now they retraced their steps a few hundred yards, and began to reconnoiter the island.

Presently Kincaid said, "It's about four o'clock. It'll be dawn pretty soon. We'll stop and rest. Better take off what clothing you can and wring it out. Especially get the water out of your boots."

They had just finished wringing their saturated clothing and had started to dress again, when there came a fresh clatter of horses' hooves and the sound of voices.

It was close to dawn now and the sky was lightening. Dimly, Matt saw the file of men on horseback passing about two or three hundred yards away.

"Sir," Carter said, crawling in closer in the tall grass. "I believe it's the platoon."

Some of the riders had ascended a bluff through a cut in the bank that was only now beginning to be visible.

"Are you sure, Mr. Carter?"

"They're wearing army uniforms, sir."

"A lot of people wear army uniforms," Kincaid said suspiciously. "Don't make a sound!"

The column approached and they could hear voices.

Kincaid leaned close to Carter's ear. "That sound like any kind of talk you can understand, Mr. Carter?"

"What is it?"

"They're hostiles. That's an old trick, dressing up in army uniforms." He looked at McBride. "Sometimes they even blow our bugle calls in reverse."

"They do, sir?" Reb's jaw dropped.

"Hell, yes. They blow retreat right in the middle of a battle. The Comanches did that once down on the Staked Plains. Confused the hell out of us till we caught on."

The column was past them now.

Kincaid stood up, but kept himself bent over as he said, "Come on. We'll ford the river now. I think the platoon's on top of that one over there. Hurry! It'll be dawn soon."

The platoon was indeed on the top of the bluff and now under the command of Sergeant Gus Olsen, assisted by Windy Mandalian. They had gotten quickly across the river and worked their way through a strip of timber and out into the open, where the men dismounted to fight on foot. Windy had ridden ahead with one of the Delaware scouts to reconnoiter the bluff.

Some of the horses had become spooked and were unmanageable, and one started racing toward the Sioux, its rider, a boy from Ohio named Colley, sawing at the reins. A volley of firing brought both Colley and his horse to the ground, the horse dead, but Colley miraculously escaping back to the soldier lines.

"Where is Lieutenant Kincaid?" demanded Windy, coming up to where Olsen was standing.

"He's cut off on the other side of the river."

"Sergeant, we'd better mount up and head for the bluff. There's a trail."

In the excitement a couple of horses got away from the horse-holders and made a break toward the Indian lines, just as Colley's mount had done, but fortunately they were without riders.

Olsen had mounted his bay; as he did so the man beside him, Private Fitzhugh, was shot through his stomach just as he was in the act of mounting his horse. He fell to the ground, and Olsen, his attention on the platoon, saw out of the corner of his eye another man dismount to help him, but the best he could do was drag him into a clump of heavy underbrush where he might not be found by the Indians.

"Soldier, leave a canteen and get moving," barked Olsen, wheeling his mount. Then, to the men around him: "It's the hill. We got to make it to the hill!"

The bluff was so steep that the horses were having difficulty carrying their riders to the top. Olsen urged them on, and when he finally reached the others, he found that Windy had secured an excellent position from which the men were able to fire down on the Sioux. Though outnumbered, they easily held their own, and presently the firing died down.

Now, as night settled in, the men of Easy Company

waited. Fitzhugh had been left below, hidden from the Sioux, they hoped; in any case, he was not expected to live. Weller had been shot in the neck but was resting well, while two others had suffered minor wounds.

"Except for that poor bastard Fitzhugh, we're damn lucky—so far," Olsen said to Windy.

"They'll probably try one more time when it's light," the scout said. "But they may try an ambush after we pull out; that's always a possibility."

The scout squinted at the lightening sky now, as dawn started up behind the horizon. He was just about to speak again when there came a crash of rifle fire from the bottom of the hill.

A sudden silence fell, and now they all heard the familiar voice of Matt Kincaid.

"Sergeant Olsen, we are at direct four o'clock from your position toward the river. Fire at will! We've got 'em boxed!"

Sergeant Ben Cohen sat behind his desk—like a hungry lion in his lair, Corporal Bradshaw thought—glaring at the two young men standing before him.

"Are we going to be court-martialed, Sergeant?" the one on the left asked coolly. And Bradshaw felt his stomach tighten.

"I wouldn't be that easy on you, myself," Cohen said, and his eyes were glittering.

It was the other one—Walt—who seemed a little less rigid. And now he said, "We are sorry, Sergeant, but we have tidied up the barracks. My brother and I were just funning a bit and it got out of hand."

"'Out of hand' behavior is not what we expect in an army post, mister. You are guests of Captain Conway, and as such you are expected to behave yourselves."

"We said we were sorry." Will looked vastly bored.

A long sigh took its time circulating through the first

sergeant's massive frame. All his muscles seemed to relax for a moment and he folded his hands across his chest, twiddling his thumbs as he raised his eyes toward the ceiling of the orderly room—evidently seeking support from Above.

Still with his eyes on Higher Forces, the sergeant began to speak. Meanwhile, Four Eyes sat rooted in his chair. Only once before had he observed his superior in such an attitude, and the result had been the virtual dismemberment of a green and quite snotty second lieutenant.

"You have been here four days and three nights," Cohen began with all the solemnity of a preacher at graveside. "And you have—one—entered the officers' mess hall without permission; two—almost set fire to the supply room by smoking and drinking there against regulations; three—gambled, also against company regulations. Yes—" He held up an enormous palm to stay any rebuttal. "Yes, I know some of the men do engage in cards from time to time for their relaxation. But with you, most of them have lost their entire pay. They have since been assigned to various special details that I reserve for such infractions of the regulations and such disrespect. Unfortunately"—and at this point his eye fell on Four Eyes, who was trembling with fear that the sergeant might have learned about his own participation in the action—" unfortunately the two of you are not enlisted in the United States Army, and therefore do not fall under these regulations. *But*"—and he leaned forward suddenly, bringing his great eyes and teeth to bear right on the two standing before him—"But I will promise you something." He stopped and leaned back in his chair, his arms braced against the desk, as he eyed them through slitted lids, while a wicked look spread into his face.

"What's that, Sergeant?" Will asked innocently; and Four Eyes felt the needle in the words.

"I think, instead of telling you, I'll demonstrate," Ben Cohen said, rising slowly to his feet.

Four Eyes almost couldn't stand it; he was shaking. It was when the top kick was quiet, with soft voice and gentle movements, that he was at his most terrifying.

"Corporal."

"Yes, Sergeant!"

"You may accompany us to the rear of the orderly room."

"Right, Sergeant!"

"And Corporal—"

"Yes, Sergeant!"

"—I will require a hammer and a ladder."

"Right, Sergeant!"

It was late afternoon, but there was still enough light to see the great height of the sky, and this Four Eyes did, wondering what the hell Cohen was up to. The rear of the orderly room was where he usually meted out physical discipline to any recalcitrants who failed to understand army rules and regulations. And the big knuckles, the cordlike arms and shoulders of Ben Cohen, gave testimony to his ability. To date, no man had ever stood up to Easy Company's "first shirt." One or two, twenty years younger, had come close—but still they'd landed hard on their asses, wiser than they had been.

Bradshaw moved close to the sergeant; he was fearful, but he felt that he had to remind his superior that if he laid hands on a civilian he would be skewered on a spit and roasted over a high flame. And where would that leave Easy Company? But he held his tongue. The Sarge—the Sarge, by God, knew what he was doing. He had to. But was he *really* going to beat up on those two monsters?

The party of four walked quickly around to the back of the orderly room, where they were out of sight of anyone else on the post.

"It's getting to be dark," Sergeant Cohen observed. "And it *will* be dark soon. Gets dark out here every night, you know."

Four Eyes saw the twins watching him with suspicion, unable to figure out what he was driving at. Cohen had picked up a piece of lumber that was leaning against the building, and now stood it straight on end with the top against the eave and the other end straight down on the hard-packed ground.

Pointing to three large rocks that the last recipient of disciplinary action had dug out of a six-by-six hole in the ground, he said, "Corporal, move those rocks over to the board so it holds the bottom firm, and brace it against the building with that other piece of lumber there." He pointed. "You boys want to help him, you can." His usual gravel voice was laced with honey now.

The twins looked at each other, and in unison they shrugged and walked over to the big rocks. Now, with Four Eyes, they secured the board. Then Bradshaw fetched a ladder and a hammer and nails, and Cohen told him to secure the top end of the heavy board to the log roof.

The sergeant tried it to see that it was firm. "Solid, would you young fellers say?"

"Looks it." Again they looked at one another, and there was a smirk in Walt's face, a sneer at Will's mouth. But Four Eyes saw that the look on Sergeant Cohen's face was absolutely wicked. He was relishing every second of it. Four Eyes looked at the boys, and he almost felt sorry for them; they both looked so thin and pale.

Sergeant Ben Cohen stood before the twins. "Now then, I'll reveal to you two young fellers my surprise. This here board, it is tough. Doubt you could cut it easy.

And as you see, it is heavy, hard. Harder'n a man's head or body, huh? Now, as the corporal here knows, and as you young fellers have reminded me, I cannot put army discipline on you." He paused. "That right, Corporal Bradshaw?"

"Right, Sarge."

"Right?" He looked directly at the twins.

They nodded. "That is correct."

"That is correct, Sergeant."

"I am glad you fellers understand army regulations so well." Cohen looked at the sky, at the edge of the orderly room building, where the shadows were lengthening. He looked down at the toe of his right boot.

"It gets real dark here, like I said. Man trips over something, runs into somethin', coming out to take a leak, he don't know what it is. And they ain't nobody around to tell him." He grinned, blinked at the boys, and stepped over to the board.

"No spring in that board either, is there?" he said, trying it with his great paws.

And now Four Eyes stared in disbelief as he watched the sergeant take a red bandanna out of his hip pocket and wrap it tightly around the knuckles of his right hand. He held up his fist for the three of them to see. Four Eyes immediately thought of a Sioux war club.

Without a word, Ben Cohen stepped closer to the piece of thick, heavy lumber, and put his hands down at his sides. He waited, letting the breath go out of his body. Now he raised his hands, still relaxed. There didn't seem to be a tense muscle in his body. He waited another moment, and then, like a striking snake, his right fist, bandaged in the red bandanna, flew out and smashed into the board. His fist, meeting the board, sounded like the crash of musketry. The board broke cleanly in two.

He stood back, not even drawing extra breath as he surveyed his handiwork and then his fist. "My, my, I'd sure hate to get hit with one of them things," he said, his eyes still on his bandaged fist. Unwrapping his hand, the sergeant carefully folded his red bandanna and returned it to his hip pocket.

"Corporal Bradshaw, the two civilians will clean up the detail—under your supervision."

"Yes, Sergeant."

Ben Cohen hummed a pleasant tune to himself as he walked into the orderly room.

Captain Conway, coming out of his office, was struck by something in his top kick's demeanor. "Cohen, you look like you just swallowed a canary," he said.

"Yes, sir. Make that two canaries, Captain."

It took Conway a second or two to catch it, and then he grinned. "Ben, I still haven't figured out how to tell those two apart. Have you?"

"No, sir, I haven't." And then, as the captain put his hand on the doorknob to go out, Cohen said, "Sir?"

Conway turned, waiting.

The first sergeant was standing in front of his desk, and Conway suddenly noticed that his right hand was quite red and seemed a bit swollen.

"If I may say so, sir... I don't give a shit."

And with that sore hand, Ben Cohen snapped the captain a smart salute.

eight

"I'm so glad to meet you boys, finally." It was Flora Conway speaking, as she showed Will and Walt Kenning into her living room. "Of course, the captain has mentioned you, and I caught a glimpse or two, and now...well." She smiled, and her smile included not only the two boys but Edwina Carter and Maggie Cohen.

"Well, we have heard of you too, ma'am." Walt said, his Georgia accent strong as he seated himself next to his twin brother.

"I hope you like tea," Flora said, seating herself on the horsehair sofa her husband had ordered from Cheyenne at considerable expense. "Edwina, come sit beside me, dear."

"Anyhow," said Will, speaking for the first time, "we have also heard how helpful it is to the men to have ladies such as yourselves on the post. It brings a feeling of something special." And he blushed slightly, which all three ladies present found absolutely charming.

Edwina had seated herself beside Flora Conway, and was now helping to pass the filled cups. The tea service, Flora told them, was her mother's, and when she had died, she'd left it to her and the captain.

She laughed like a little girl. "Yes, I remember this tea set from when I was—well, even younger than you boys. And that was a good while ago."

Everyone laughed politely at that, with several voices—the boys' loud among them—demurring at the reflection on Flora's age.

"My husband has always teased me about what he calls my 'tea fights,'" Flora said. "And he avoids them as much as possible, but I have asked him to stop in this afternoon, if only for a moment." She looked at Will. "Sugar? Milk?"

"Thank you, ma'am."

"And you—Will, is it?"

"I'm Walt, ma'am. And yes, sugar and milk, please."

"My, you really are identical twins, aren't you?"

They all chuckled at that.

"I mean," Flora said, "not only do you look exactly alike, but you appear to eat and drink alike." And she burst into laughter at the expression on their faces. "Oh, please don't mind if I tease you a little. You—you are rather grave Southern gentlemen, are you not?"

And if softened them. As her husband had long noted, she could charm fish out of the water.

"Now you look at home, lads," Maggie Cohen said. "My husband Ben has been telling me that you've made yourselves useful around the post. I have to say, even though the captain is not here, that the post needs a different touch than only and always and forever the military."

"Well, we've learned a lot. At least I have," said Walt, with a quick look at Will. And when his twin nodded, Flora let out a gust of laughter.

"Do you really do everything alike?" It was Edwina coming in now, with her soft voice and glance.

"Just about."

"But do you ever like to be alone—each one by himself?"

"Oh, yes, ma'am. We like that a lot."

"It's still the same," Flora maintained, and this brought another round of laughter.

"I suppose people do ask all the time how it's possible to tell you apart," Edwina said.

"That they do, ma'am."

"I think I can tell you apart," she said suddenly, and she sounded just a little out of breath as she spoke.

Edwina and Will were looking at each other. Maggie Cohen shifted uncomfortably in her chair, while Flora Conway reached for the pot of tea.

"How?" Will asked. "Of course you can tell now, because we told you our names." And then he turned toward his brother. "Or did we?" he said, laughing.

"Ah, you mean you might have tricked us, even so?" Flora said gaily. "Well, we'll just have to take your word—words—for it."

"How will you tell us apart?" Will asked, his glance directly on Edwina.

"That's a secret," she said, dropping her eyes and reaching for her cup of tea.

Suddenly Flora clapped her hands. "I've a grand idea."

"Ah, and what would that be, love?" asked Maggie, always eager like a little child for games.

"If the young men are willing."

"Depends on what it is, Mrs. Conway," Walt said. And then he added quickly, with a brilliant smile, "Not that we wouldn't do anything you wanted anyway, ma'am."

"Tell us your idea, please, Flora," said Edwina, lean-

97

ing forward and clasping her hands around her knees.

"If the boys agree, they'll go in the other room and change their clothing around. Mix things up. And then when they come back, we have to tell which is which."

An excited laugh broke from the ladies, and the boys grinned, exchanging looks.

Walt nodded. "We'll give it a try," he said.

When they had left the room, Maggie looked at Edwina. "Do you really know how to tell them apart?"

"I think so."

"I'm sure I don't," Flora said. "But I'll guess anyway."

"Is guessing fair?"

"Why not?" She reflected a moment. "No," she said earnestly. "I think not. Let's make a rule. No guessing. You have to really tell from something you know."

"But you don't have to tell *how* you know," said Edwina.

"But why not, dear?"

"I don't know. I think that should be secret. After all, if one of us tells how to know them apart, maybe Will and Walt won't want that. We have to respect their wishes, don't we?"

Whatever Flora or Maggie might have said to that was cut off by the sudden appearance of Warner Conway.

"Warner, you're just in time, dear."

"Ah, I only popped in to see how things are going, my dear. Can't stay." With a nod to Maggie and Edwina Carter, he crossed the room and opened the door to the bedroom. "What in—!"

"Oh, Warner, the twins are in there."

"What are they doing in our bedroom?"

"Just changing, dear. Do sit down. We're playing a game."

"I can't stay," he protested, his eyes on the door of his bedroom.

But the three women were all over him to sit and have a cup of tea, and instantly they began telling him of Flora's proposal. The conversation was abruptly interrupted by the boys entering the room.

They had indeed changed their appearance, switching some of the clothing, combing their hair differently, and even slouching as they walked, working themselves right into Flora's game, to the delight of the ladies. Conway looked on in amazement. It was a new set of twins he was seeing.

"Let me try first," Flora said. "By the way, we've agreed among us while you were out of the room that we mustn't guess. Because just by luck someone might guess correctly."

"We had arrived at the same notion, ma'am."

Flora stared at each one in turn, and finally she simply shook her head. "I can't. I'd be guessing. I really cannot tell one of you from the other."

"I pass too," said Maggie.

"Warner, will you try, dear?"

"I pass," Conway said with a smile, entering more into the spirit of it. "I've been trying to tell them apart for five days now, and I'm still in the dark."

"Edwina, it's up to you."

All eyes were on Edwina now; the color had risen in her pale face. Everyone was watching her intently.

"I may need a moment or two."

"Take your time," Will told her.

Conway was watching her carefully as her eyes moved over each of the boys.

"We should take bets on it," Walt said, laughing. And then he looked quickly at the captain. "I mean false bets, friendly bets, sir. We, uh, know that gambling for money is against army regulations."

Conway took it in goodwill, saying, "If you were in the army, I'd bet you an overnight pass."

The captain's smooth delivery served to relieve what could have become a tense moment.

Suddenly, Edwina held the palms of her hands together in front of her and sat up straight in her chair, like a little girl.

"You're Will," she said suddenly, pointing to Will. "And you're Walt—naturally." And she brought her hands down on her knees and rocked back and forth in her seat. "Am I right?" And her eyes looked at everyone in the room.

The boys didn't answer right away, and then Conway said, "Maybe they don't know how to tell *themselves* apart." And this brought a chuckle from everyone.

"Did you guess it?" Will asked, his eyes fully on Edwina.

She was shaking her head. "No. We agreed not to just guess."

Conway stood up. "I really must get back, ladies and gentlemen. Thank you for the tea." Bending to his wife, he gave her a peck on the forehead.

After Conway had left, Will said, "Tell us how you figured that out, please."

"Oh, no—we also agreed that we would keep that a secret." And no matter how much the boys urged her to tell, she still refused.

Warner Conway walked slowly across the parade, his thoughts on the scene he had just witnessed. He too was wondering how Edwina Carter had been able to tell the twins apart, if indeed she really hadn't just guessed.

It wasn't until he was in bed that night that he was suddenly struck by the answer. Of course, he thought, wide awake now—of course. For a moment he had the urge to tell Flora, but she was asleep peacefully beside him; and in the morning he simply decided to keep the information to himself.

nine ─────────────

Fox and Two Coyotes led their band of warriors up the slope of a wide draw, heading toward a stand of timber below the rimrocks. From here it was possible to sweep the long valley with the white man's glasses. Both Fox and Two Coyotes knew that the fight with the soldiers had involved only one company; and since they had been forced to withdraw, it was clear now that if the soldiers came after them full strength, they'd be in bad trouble. They had in fact not intended to attack the soldiers, and had stumbled on them by accident, the whiskey they had taken from the wagon train having slackened their usually sharp perceptions. And when the white leader, Kincaid, had suddenly appeared at their rear with the other soldiers, they were caught in a crossfire and were lucky to escape.

Now they had pulled off the North Platte Wagon Road, which they had been following toward the Bozeman Trail, moving always with care, alternately slowly and swiftly, but eager to get well away from any possible retaliation from the full complement of bluelegs. Indeed, Fox had decided that this would be the way they would fight the soldiers. Hadn't Crazy Horse done it, and with great success?

In the shade of a tall spruce, he said so to Two Coyotes, who nodded once, grunting.

"But neither one of us is Crazy Horse," Two Coyotes said.

Fox's face darkened. "We can still make use of his way: to draw in the enemy and then to separate him from his main force, and . . ." And Fox made a slicing motion with his hand.

They were sitting cross-legged under the big spruce, on the soft, porous spring ground, with the morning sun high overhead, their eyes combing over the great valley below them as they spoke.

Two Coyotes said nothing, and Fox resumed, "Even as happened at the river with Kincaid and the other soldiers."

Two Coyotes's face showed nothing as he said, "Except that they escaped us and then came again to the other soldiers and boxed us, so we had to run away very fast."

Again, Fox's face filled with a dark scowl. He did not like—had never liked—the way Two Coyotes pointed out such uncomfortable details whenever they discussed strategy. Fox would have preferred not having Two Coyotes with him—at least as a warrior in command—and he did all he could to keep him in a subsidiary, advisory role. Without much success, however. Two Coyotes had been his boyhood friend and there were ties between them—loyalties as well as enmities, the latter mostly from Fox's side—that transcended the simple fact that now they were leading a renegade band of

102

braves in opposition to the wishes of Owl Feather and the elders.

Two Coyotes had long felt the necessity of fighting the whites, for he had vowed that he would die a warrior rather than live like a dog. Yet he was of a different temperament than his friend, who was headstrong and a bully. Once he had told Fox that he needed an advisor such as himself. "Otherwise you will rush in too quickly and you will be lost." But Fox, being what he was, a young man seeking power, had swept the advice aside. Yet he knew that Two Coyotes was right, so he maintained the relationship with him. He relied much more on Two Coyotes than he would ever have admitted.

They had made camp in the stand of timber. It was a good site, where no one could approach without being seen. It had been a long, hard ride and now the braves were resting. Some had fallen asleep, some were smoking and talking quietly.

Fox and Two Coyotes did not sleep; they sat under the spruce tree and discussed what they would do.

Beneath them stretched the great valley of the Greybull. In the morning light the colors of the land were myriad, the valley winding down to the plain from which they had come, with the river flashing through dense stands of cottonwood and box elder. And above where they were sitting, and across the valley, rose the immutable rimrocks as far as the eye or the soldier-glasses could see, the great buttes and ridges thrusting into the endless azure sky. Now a lone eagle swept in a wide arc above their heads.

Two Coyotes said, "We cannot defeat the white man. He is too many. It is as Owl Feather and the others have long told it."

Fox grunted in strong dissatisfaction. "You talk like an old man."

"Would that I had the old man's wisdom," Two Coyotes said. "But hear this, my friend. You know I have fought the whites; and so I will continue to do until the end. I am telling the truth that is staring at us."

"We must never stop fighting," Fox said.

And Two Coyotes nodded. "It is only that we must fight wisely, my friend. I say this because you have not learned what I told you long ago—to ponder before you act."

"One does not always have time for pondering."

"That is true, but unfortunate."

Now, unexpectedly, their conversation was cut short by the sudden appearance of a warrior riding up the draw toward where they sat. They were out of sight, but the warrior—Falling Man—had been told by Two Coyotes where to find them.

Falling Man rode up fast.

Fox looked at him in surprise, wondering what he had ridden in for when he was supposed to be watching their backtrail.

Slipping down from his pony, Falling Man approached on foot, and spoke with his eyes on Two Coyotes.

"I see no soldiers. Many Names looked too, with the soldier-glasses, and they are none. We went as far back as the crossing of the river where Runs Laughing had the bad stomach."

Two Coyotes looked at him thoughtfully, feeling Fox's eyes on his face in surprise and anger at not knowing about the reconnaissance.

"It is good," Fox said, stepping in to assert his authority and leadership. "Stay there with Many Names," he added; and he felt better when Falling Man turned immediately, without looking at Two Coyotes, and mounted his pony.

When he had ridden away, Two Coyotes said, "So they are not following."

"It is good," Fox said.

"Maybe. Maybe the soldier leader has spoken on the Singing Wire to soldiers at the fort up ahead on the Bozeman."

"Ah, but that fort is empty," said Fox. "It is the fort the soldier chief Carrington left when Red Cloud beat him." He looked up at the sun. "The fort where Crazy Horse rubbed out all the bluelegs."

Two Coyotes's face remained impassive. "We do not know. Soldiers could be there again. We must be careful."

"We will send scouts to see. The American trader at Pine Creek said the fort was burned."

Two Coyotes took a while to say anything to that. "Maybe," he said finally, but Fox could see that his thoughts were on something else.

"Maybe the soldiers go to their camp to get more soldiers to come fight with us," Two Coyotes said.

Fox was annoyed at his second-in-command having the thought he himself had just reached, but hadn't been quick enough to express in words.

"For they will come after us," Two Coyotes said. He looked out at the long valley with the sun sparkling on it. "They always do," he said.

"We will ambush them," Fox said. "We can find places for that purpose."

He looked at Two Coyotes, seeing that the other's eyes were closed.

"Let us smoke," Two Coyotes said.

"We should go back quickly," said Fox.

But Two Coyotes insisted. "We must smoke first. It is the way of it."

Fox wanted more than anything else to rouse the camp

and ride off quickly to set up the ambush, but the words uttered by Two Coyotes would not let him.

Now as the sun rose to the zenith of the great sky, they prepared their smoke, doing everything in the ritual manner so that all would be pure, and the decision good.

All this time, Two Coyotes had kept his eyes closed, even while preparing the smoke. Fox knew that he was trying to dream. He knew that while Two Coyotes was not a medicine man, he had powerful dreams. He knew that sometimes Two Coyotes could *see*.

Two Coyotes did not open his eyes, nor did he speak until the two of them had smoked. The sun was very hot, and its heat lanced through the branches of the spruce under which they sat. Still, Two Coyotes did not move. The heat did not seem to affect him; but Fox had rivulets of water running down his face, neck, and back.

At last, when the smoke was finished, Two Coyotes spoke. "We will go back," he said. "But not to where the soldiers ride to their camp."

"Where, then?" asked Fox.

"They have not ridden back to their camp," Two Coyotes said.

"Where, then?"

"To the People," Two Coyotes said. "To Owl Feather's band."

"But that is foolish."

"The soldiers are going there," Two Coyotes said. He stood up. "They go in peace," he said, "but we go in war."

"It is good," Fox said after a moment. "Maybe more young men will join us when they see that we are strong."

"Now we must return to our first plan," Two Coyotes said.

"But we had decided we were too few, and the Look-Likes could not be trusted."

"There is a way." Two Coyotes looked out across the

106

gleaming valley. "There is Long Horse. The Hunkpapa young men are also restless."

"Betcha!" Will said with a laugh. "Betcha that Dragoon Colt."

"No!" Walt shook his head. "Not that. It cost me too much."

"Not any more than mine did."

"I mean, it cost me keeping it out of the clutches of that son of a bitch Fox."

They both laughed at that. "Boy, if he ever found out it was his own squaw hid it—"

"You'd have been torn in a million pieces."

The boys were sitting on the railing at one end of the post paddock. It was evening and they had just finished sweeping the mess hall after supper, and were enjoying the relaxation of a smoke and the comparison of notes on their adventures.

"So what will you bet?" Will asked after a moment. "If that .44 is so damn precious to you, you'd better get up something pretty good."

His brother thought for a moment and then said, "I'll bet you the shuffle Professor Joliet taught me."

Will stared at him, his mouth dropping open. "You're on!"

"And you're on," laughed Walt.

"No time limit?"

"You've got to do it before we get out of here."

"And if I don't?"

"Then I want that diamond you got in the game at Leadville."

Will nodded. "Right you are." He grinned, and then shook his head ruefully. "That poor old miner never even suspected I was second-dealing him."

"I think we have to go easy here," Walt said. "That son of a bitch Cohen doesn't like us."

107

His brother released a great roar of laughter. "What ever gave you that notion!"

They fell silent then, as the sun moved swiftly down to the edge of the sky; each was contemplating the daring bet proposed by Will Kenning.

"She's a mighty good-looking woman," Walt said after a long moment.

"She is that." Will sighed as he said the words, his breath catching.

"Do you really think they put her up to all those questions she's been asking?"

"I'm sure of it. Of course, you know women are always filled with curiosity anyway. But they are famous for being the cat that catches the mouse. And that Kincaid is no dummy."

"Nor is the good captain," Walt put in.

"Nor is the captain, or that crazy hairy buckskin scout."

"The only thing is, we've got to have our stories together. I know they've been trying to trip us; and you, you horse's ass, you really screwed it when you told them we'd been with the Sioux since September."

"October, I told them."

"So? I'd already told them January."

"So, we were frightened. We're kids. Right? So we got the dates wrong."

Will added. "And I know for sure I was frightened. Thank God they're more crazy about gambling than lifting scalps."

"Thank God for Uncle Milburn," said Walt. "All I can say is, I hope between him and Professor Joliet we'll be able to get out of here and back to civilization."

"Well, we need a clear eye and a steady hand," Will said. "Just like our teachers taught. Am I right?"

"Right." Walt agreed. "But remember they were talking about civilized games in civilized places like saloons, riverboats, and sporting houses. Hell, here we've been honking around with a bunch of crazy redskins and the U.S. Army out in God's country."

"We've got to really think about getting out," Will said, sobering suddenly. "It might be tough if we get sent to the regimental fort."

"Well, you know there's one way," Walt said.

His brother was silent, his eyes on the prairie sweeping before them. After a long moment he said, "Well, it might be the only way."

Walt looked at him now. "Will, you haven't forgotten our reason for coming out West."

His brother looked down. "No. I haven't." In a moment he raised his eyes to meet his brother's. "I hate them just as much as you do. Maybe more."

"We must never forget that," Walt said earnestly. His jaw was set as he stared out across the rapidly darkening land. "It's a good way of evening up some of the score with the filthy swine!"

"The difficulty," Will said, "is in not giving it away."

"I know. You've got to watch your temper, and that damn humor of yours. Be more innocent. Do everything they want. Anything!" Walt watched the grin start on his twin's face.

"Shit, that's what I am doing, ain't I, brother? I'm letting her do anything she wants."

All the seriousness had suddenly left them now as Walt matched his brother's wide grin. "The diamond against the Professor's shuffle." And he added, "You'd better get moving. You know that patrol could get back anytime."

"By the time we get away from here," Will said. "That's the condition."

Walt nodded. "I was just thinking . . ." he said pensively.

"About what?" Will reached into the pocket of his

hickory shirt and took out two cheroots and passed one of them to his twin brother.

"I was thinking about Uncle Milburn and the Professor."

Will had struck a match on the rail near his leg, and held it for Walt. They were silent while they smoked for a moment.

Then Will said, "We'll go back there, won't we?"

Walt said nothing for a long moment. When he finally spoke, his voice seemed far away. "Where? Go back . . . where?"

The two boys sat on the paddock fence for a long while as the sky darkened into night. They were no longer laughing. They were reminding themselves of why they had come West, and what they were going to do.

ten _____

Windy Mandalian's battered stock saddle was the envy of every man in Easy Company. The scout, being a civilian, was permitted his own horse, saddle, and firearms; and of course, no one but a maniac would have deliberately preferred a McClellan, with its split saddle seat that caused untold hours of agony to cavalry and mounted infantry alike. His little blue roan, easygoing and hardbitten like himself, was as much a part of his outfit as was his Springfield, his Colt Dragoon, his bowie knife, not to mention the ever-present cut of chewing tobacco. Without that big wad in his cheek, Windy would have looked out of uniform.

Matt Kincaid watched him now as he walked his roan back down the trail. After the fight at the river crossing, they had started out in two columns. The casualty count following the encounter with Fox and Two Coyotes had been Fitzhugh dead, Weller shot in the neck, and two men of the third squad with flesh wounds. Kincaid's shoulder wound was minimal, and he had all but forgotten it save for an occasional twinge when he made a sudden move.

It was essential to press on toward Owl Feather's camp, so Matt sent Fitzhugh's body and the wounded Weller back to the post with Malone and a detail; the two men with minor wounds asked to stay with the platoon.

But they hadn't covered much distance when the messenger sent by Owl Feather met them and rode before them, escorting them to where the old chief and those of his tribe who had not ridden out with Fox and Two Coyotes waited.

When Carter rode up, Matt said, "Mr. Carter, we will break out the colors, and you may also alert McBride." It was the first Matt had spoken to First Platoon's leader since the Oglallas had decided they'd had enough and withdrawn.

"Yes, sir!" Carter snapped a salute and rode off to give the commands.

"Ride in with a big show, that's the way," Windy observed. Then he said, "I put out extra scouts, just in case Fox and Two Coyotes takes a notion."

"I think they were as surprised as we were, running into us like that."

"Happens. Hell, anything can happen out in this here country," Windy observed.

"And you are figuring Owl Feather is still on the square, are you?"

The scout nodded. "I know him a good while, Matt. Besides, he ain't dumb. He knows damn well what would happen to him if he tried anything now."

"That's how I see it," agreed Kincaid. "Just wanted to check. Sometimes a man can outfigure himself. Especially when he's gone without sleep."

They were silent, listening to the creak of saddle

leather, the jangle of the horses' bits, an occasional murmur among the men. Off to the left now, they heard Carter barking orders.

"That green dude you got there sure is a ball-buster," Windy observed slowly. "Wants to whip Mr. Lo all by his lonesome."

Kincaid sighed. "We get 'em."

And they fell silent again until Carter came riding up, pulling his horse to an abrupt stop in front of Matt and Windy, who had stopped to take a look ahead through the field glasses.

"You don't want your horse to leave it all on the trail, do you, Lieutenant?" drawled Windy.

Carter flushed slightly, but ignored the scout's remark. "Sir," he said, turning to Kincaid. "Can we trust this messenger? I'm sure you've thought of it, sir. But I did think I ought to mention it."

"I have thought of that, Mr. Carter, just as you say," Matt replied, slipping the field glasses back into their case, and kneeing his mount forward.

"It could be a trap, sir."

"It could be."

"I mean, if I may say so, sir, we were caught by surprise back there at the river."

"So was Mr. Lo, Lieutenant."

Windy had walked his horse away, intending to check the getaway men, and now Carter drew up alongside Kincaid.

"Sir . . ."

"Yes, Mr. Carter."

"I wanted to say something, sir. I wanted to apologize for my action back at the river crossing. I—I guess I lost my temper."

"You made a mistake that could have cost some lives, mister. We were lucky. What about next time?"

"There won't be a next time, sir."

113

A harsh laugh fell from Matt. "Oh, yes, there will be a next time. You are what you are, soldier, and you aren't going to change that easily. You are arrogant, impatient, bad-tempered—all of which, added together, means you're stupid."

Carter had flushed scarlet.

"Sir, I know I deserve what you say. I only want to fight the Indians; and all we seem to do is ride around and drill and talk about how wonderful the poor red man is. I'm sorry, sir," he went on quickly, seeing how he was beginning to get emotional again. "I just can't see this catering to the enemy."

"Nobody's catering to anyone, mister. You don't seem to realize that the rules out here are not like any rules anywhere else. We don't make the rules. The army doesn't make the rules. Not by a long shot. The country itself makes the rules, and like it or not, the Indians are part of that country." He paused, looking at Carter, remembering something he'd been meaning to speak about that had slipped to the back of his mind until just now.

"Mr. Carter, Sergeant Cohen informed me that you told him you wanted Private Evans placed on some shit details. Is that correct? I meant to speak to you about it back at the post, but we left in a hurry."

"Yes, sir, it's true. Evans . . . well, he was rude—rude to myself and to Mrs. Carter."

"Rude? I know Evans. He doesn't appear to be the rude type to me. How was he rude?"

"It's . . . it's his attitude, sir."

"Sergeant Cohen told me you threatened Evans with the guardhouse."

"I told him that was what he deserved, sir. Maybe I was hasty, sir."

"Lieutenant, I don't have to tell you Outpost Nine is not West Point. We need all the men on active duty that we can get. That doesn't mean we let anyone run over us, but it does mean we bend a little here and there." He paused, guiding his horse away from Carter as he moved in close and their stirrups and boots touched. "What was the real reason, Mr. Carter? Why were you so angry at Evans that you wanted him locked up or put on some shit detail?"

But the conversation was interrupted at this point, as the Oglalla messenger sent by Owl Feather came riding back down the trail. As if from nowhere, Windy Mandalian appeared, and now Kincaid kicked his horse forward to see what was up.

"Village up ahead." The Oglalla spoke in English, but used his hands also.

"Good enough," said Matt.

"Best if you and me ride in first, I think," Windy said.

Matt hesitated. That would leave Carter in charge of the platoon, with the creek between them. It gave him an uncomfortable feeling.

"What is it, Matt?"

"It's Carter."

"I gotcha. But you need to talk to Owl Feather, and I better be there, since we're old buddies."

"Shit," said Kincaid. But then his face cleared. Turning to McBride, he said, "Tell Sergeant Olsen I want him, Reb."

It was about the middle of the afternoon when Matt and Windy rode into the ring of tipis. Ignoring the sullen silence that prevailed, and that was quite the opposite of the usual Indian camp, they followed the Oglalla messenger to Owl Feather's lodge. Matt spotted it easily, by its central location and by the tattered American flag that hung from one of its poles. There was no movement of wind and the flag hung limp, still a sign that Owl Feather and his people were at peace with the whites.

Matt and Windy walked their horses into the camp

115

slowly. There were children here and there, but they were not playing; they were quiet and staying close to their mothers.

"The friendlies are not exactly friendly, are they?" Matt observed laconically to his companion.

Windy said nothing, but moved his chew to the other side of his mouth.

Matt observed the scene carefully, without appearing to notice a thing; he knew Windy was doing the same. Yes, Owl Feather was off the reservation, but not far off, and he was showing his flag, and he had sent a runner for them. The Sioux, like any of the tribes, paid little heed to such matters as boundary lines. It was not in their nature to stay in one place, and the army of the Kincaids and Conways could allow a little latitude as long as there was no real trouble.

But there were always men like Carter, bigots who held unreasoning hatred for Indians, hostile or friendly. "The only good Indian is a dead Indian," Phil Sheridan had said, and insecure young hotshots of Carter's ilk were more than willing to take that tragically silly motto as their anthem.

Therefore, Kincaid had given Carter specific orders to be followed in his absence, and he had also instructed Sergeant Olsen to "assist" the young lieutenant in carrying out those orders. This made Kincaid feel slightly more secure; he knew Olsen wasn't likely to take any shit from some bushy-tailed West Pointer.

At a signal from their escort they drew rein and dismounted. As he and Windy entered Owl Feather's tipi, Matt could feel the unseen eyes of the Oglala encampment frimly fixed on his back.

"But do you *really mean* that you and your brother were only eleven?" Edwina gasped as she stared in amazement at Will Kenning, who was seated across from her. They were in her quarters having tea, after Sergeant Cohen, following Captain Conway's suggestion, had sent Will to put up a shelf over Mrs. Carter's stove.

"That's right, ma'am." Will almost smiled as he watched the utter surprise in Edwina's face.

"And you—both of you—actually were under fire!" She sat on the edge of the horsehair sofa, her fingers touching her cheek in disbelief. "But you were hardly—well, you were still *babies!*"

Will could no longer contain himself, and he burst into laughter. "Forgive me, do forgive me, ma'am."

"It's all right. But I don't see how you can laugh. You were both children! Going to war like that. Some of you could have been killed."

"Some of us were, ma'am," Will said, and he was suddenly dead sober, the laughter dying on his face as he even paled and his lips tightened at the memory. "There were a lot of us who put on uniforms during the last weeks and months of the War." His eyes were far away. "And that was only the beginning, ma'am."

Edwina stared at him, still finding it hard to believe. Then she remembered Captain Conway warning her to listen very carefully to whatever either of the twins told her and to give him a full report. She had asked him if he didn't trust the boys, and he had said no, it wasn't that; it was that they had both been through a terrible ordeal and might even have lost a part of their memory. Anyhow, he had asked her cooperation—which, of course, she had been only too glad to give.

"And after," she said, reaching for the teapot. "What then? You went back to your home?"

Will was leaning forward in his chair with his forearms on his knees, his fingers laced together, looking down at his thumbs. Edwina saw that he was absolutely immobile as he spoke.

"We went home," he said, and she could barely hear

117

his words. "Only there wasn't any home."

"Oh, you poor boys . . ." Without realizing it, Edwina reached out and touched his arm.

Will raised his head and looked at her. "You're very kind, Mrs. Carter."

"No. You poor boys have been through too much." Edwina could not hold his gaze, and her eyes dropped. She had seen the tears starting in his eyes, and then she had seen something else. "More tea?" she asked.

"Yes, please."

They were both silent while she poured.

Edwina put down the teapot and said, "Well, what did you do then? I mean, you told me before about . . . about not finding your parents. But what then? You decided to come and explore the West?"

"More or less," Will said, brightening.

"But you couldn't have had any money. How did you manage?"

"Well," said Will, and there was a small smile playing around his mouth, "there was the family treasure. And there was our Uncle Milburn and his friend Professor Joliet."

"But I thought you said your family had all . . . disappeared."

"Ah, but Uncle Milburn isn't our real uncle. We just call him Uncle."

"And was Professor—what was his name?—a real professor?"

Both of them had returned to their former good humor, and both found the light tone infectious.

"Professor Joliet? Oh, I don't know. I don't know what he was a professor *of,* but he knew just about everything, and what he didn't know, Uncle Milburn knew. So we had an excellent education."

"And the family treasure?"

"Silver, jewelry—buried so the Yankees wouldn't get

118

it." He paused, but the dark mood didn't take over, and he went on. "We outfitted ourselves at New Orleans—guns, clothes, all that—then took the steamboat up to Kansas City, where we bought horses and headed for the Great American West." He reached for his cup of tea, feeling her eyes on the side of his face.

"My, how exciting it all sounds. But weren't either of you afraid? I'm sorry to go on so, and I don't mean any offense, but you are so young."

For a long moment they looked at each other. It was almost as though there had been an echo to her words and they were each listening to it.

"Young?" Now there was laughter in his eyes as he said, "I may be young, ma'am, but I'm a man. I've been to war. I've fought the Indians, and, uh . . . I've done my share of manly things."

"Oh, please, I meant no offense. I was . . . well, I was concerned. That's all."

Edwina felt the color coming into her face as they looked at each other now. And the more she tried to control it, the more she felt its effect. Heavens, what would he think? So young? A boy? But he was indeed a young man, she thought, as he knelt down beside her and put his head in her lap.

eleven ⸻⸻⸻⸻⸻

They entered the tipi quietly, having removed their weapons, and they took the places offered them, moving in the proper direction, with awareness of the necessary ritual. Windy, of course, knew the way of it, and he was able to indicate to Matt, who was sensitive enough to pick it up from moment to moment.

With Owl Feather were the elders of the band, old men like himself who had known the Shining Times, the days of the buffalo hunt and the wars with the Crow. Matt wondered how many of them had been at the Little Big Horn when Custer had been rubbed out.

"It'll take time," Windy had warned him. "It always takes time."

"I remember from last summer."

They smoked and waited, and then the chief spoke.

"Hear what is in my heart, and tell the Father in Washington. We will not fight the white man. We have touched the pen, and now we do as the white man wishes."

121

"What about Fox and Two Coyotes?" Kincaid asked. "They are part of your band."

"They have been counseled against their headstrong ways, but they do not hear the old men. These you see here in my lodge, and outside in our camp, these are the Oglallas who are peaceful. We have no wish to fight the white man. We have put away our weapons of war. We wish to live in peace, to hunt, to die here where our life is, and where our forefathers lie."

"Then you know nothing of Fox's plans. Do you know about the two white young men, the boys who were captured in a wagon fight last winter?" Windy said.

Owl Feather was silent a moment; he never answered in a hurry. "Yes, I know them," he replied finally. "They were with us after the wagon fight." He looked around the semicircle of warriors. "They play the cards and the little stones."

"The dice?" Windy grinned. "That's what I hear. Did they clean you out, Chief?"

A smile touched the eyes of the old man. And now he nodded slowly. "They are very quick. But we had good games." He looked at the other old men. "I think we learned from them. I hope they learned from us."

"What did you try to teach them?" Matt asked.

"We tried to teach them to become men, for they were already old. But it is not easy with the whites. Your men are always boys." Owl Feather shook his head once. "No, we were not able to teach them."

He looked off somewhere, as though recollecting, and then he said, "Then Fox and Two Coyotes took them when they went to the place where your soldiers were— the little fort. And I have not seen them now. Nor have I seen Fox and Two Coyotes and the young warriors."

Windy said, "Is that all you can tell us? You know where those two might be headed for? Fox and Two Coyotes?"

"I do not know. For they wish to fight. And they made it dangerous for our women and children."

"Do you know if they're planning to link up with any of Sitting Bull's people?" Matt asked.

"I do not know. Maybe, if they think of having a war against the whites. But then, if they only want to count coup for their bravery, they may stay alone." He paused. "Sitting Bull is in the Grandmother's Land, far away."

"But there are still some Hunkpapa around here," Windy said.

The old man was seated on a buffalo robe, and now he reached under one of its folds and brought forth a deck of playing cards. There was an appreciative murmur from the other Sioux.

Windy chuckled. He had played with the chief more than once over the years, and knew that like many Indians, he had a passion for games and gambling.

"I cut for high card," Owl Feather said. "You bet."

"Sure," Windy said. He had always been lucky with Owl Feather.

But this time it was different. The Oglalla won three times in a row, relieving Windy of money, some beads he had in his shirt pocket, and an extra skinning knife. All to the delight of the other Oglallas and the amusement of Matt Kincaid.

"You have for sure improved your technique," Windy said in rueful admiration. "Maybe I better practice up a little."

Kincaid laughed, thinking of the twins. "See, Owl Feather, now you know for real that the Indian can learn from the white man."

His remark was followed by an appreciative chorus of laughter from the old men.

As they were leaving, Matt looked directly at the old chief and said, "Why didn't Fox and Two Coyotes kill the boys? They wiped out everybody else."

Owl Feather had risen to his feet and he stood tall before them. He was silent a moment. Then he said, "The two Look-Likes are special. In some tribes they are considered as holy beings. Whether or not Fox and Two Coyotes believe this, I do not know; but perhaps they were not taking chances."

"It's true," Windy said as they rode back to the patrol. "They more'n likely do figure them for holy—something like that."

"I don't think there's much disagreement with that," Matt said. "They're holy, all right." He smiled sardonically. "Holy terrors."

Solemnly, Dennis Carter rode his horse along the column after once again being chewed out by Kincaid and dryly instructed by Sergeant Gus Olsen, with his damned "with all due respect, sir," and positively blistered by Windy Mandalian for even suggesting they go looking for Fox and Two Coyotes instead of returning to the post.

Carter knew he took himself much too seriously. He realized he had never been a popular man. Yes, he knew he was handsome, and he'd never had trouble with women, at least as far as conquest went. But he had no friends. He was lonely, and he longed to be popular and admired, as his older brother had been. Certainly he had no friends at Outpost Number Nine, and he had hoped to change that situation by an act or two of heroism under fire. He dreamed of showing that he was indispensable to the command, and a hero—not only to his fellow officers, but to the men, and most assuredly to Edwina.

There was, on the other hand, nothing unpopular about Edwina. Everyone liked her. Not that she was very outgoing. Certainly she was no Flora Conway, adored by everyone without exception, but she was very much liked. Men were especially attracted to her, for they found in her a childishness that they felt the need to educate. Carter smiled to himself at the thought, for Edwina had nothing childish about her. Rather, she was a thoroughly capable young lady. The only thing he objected to was the fact that she *was* so damned attractive to men. She was, indeed, not a little flirtatious, a quality for which he had taken her to task. Not that she ever *did* anything...

Now, in the morning sunrise as they rode toward Outpost Number Nine, he felt again the sick stroking of his jealousy. That damned Evans. The way she had looked at him. God, she could positively massage a man with those velvet eyes. Yes, he had acted badly, had spoken to the man in a nasty tone of voice, only because of his own vicious jealousy. And all Edwina had done was smile at the wretched man for carrying in some heavy object for her! Of course, Evans had also not properly executed an order, but he had done it.

And Kincaid! His eyes moved up toward the middle of the column where he could see Kincaid's back riding straight, the epitome of command. Yes, yes, he was jealous of Kincaid too! But then, hadn't he been wildly jealous of Ferguson, his older brother, a captain under Grant and a hero at Richmond? God, yes! Ferguson. It had always been, "Oh, you're Ferguson's brother, are you..."

They had just reached a place called Horsehead Crossing, and Kincaid had signaled a halt to let the horses blow, and also so they could drink where the river was shallow. They were deep along the valley of the Greybull now, with the land greening all around them and the cottonwoods shiny in the sunlight. It was a brilliant day, and looking back to the west, toward the mountains, Carter felt something pull inside his chest, and there came a stinging in his eyes.

Ah, shit, he thought. Shit! And he bit hard on his lower lip, letting his eyes drop to his horse's mane. And

125

he was suddenly back years ago in Virginia, the day Ferguson had been roaching the big sorrel's mane—Condor, his name was, and he had four white stockings—and he had asked to help. Ferguson had laughed, saying no, he was too small, too inexperienced, too young; but he had insisted, and so his big brother had given in. Millicent had been there too, watching with her younger sister Alison; and so Ferguson had let him hold Condor's halter rope. Suddenly Condor had spooked at something or other. One of the girls had screamed and Dennis had dropped the rope as the big horse reared and came down again with thrashing hooves—and he had run terrified into the stable. Ferguson had simply grabbed the halter rope and easily pacified the frightened animal. The girls had loved it, had been thrilled by it, and seemed never to stop telling about it—how little Dennis had run away terrified and how Ferguson had calmly finished roaching the big horse's mane by himself.

And he knew it wasn't that he was a coward. He wasn't; he had proven himself a number of times. It was that somehow he was afraid of Ferguson. He spent almost all his time trying to please him, to emulate him; for Ferguson was as popular as Dennis was not. And it was truly humiliating.

The water at Horsehead Crossing was sweet to the taste, and both horses and men drank their fill. Carter had dismounted and walked a few steps, leading his horse to take a look at some sagebrush growing out of a rock. Bending now, he sniffed the sharp odor of the sage and then broke off a piece and was just putting it in his pocket when he heard a step behind him.

"I have a liking for sagebrush myself," said Matt Kincaid.

"I thought my wife might like some, sir."

"Some ladies like to put it in their drawer with handkerchiefs," Matt said.

126

"How is your shoulder, sir?"

"Fine. Good as new."

A wry chuckle fell suddenly from Carter. "I'm afraid my wound is not healing so well, sir."

And when Matt's eyebrows raised in question, Carter said, "My wounded pride. I still feel like the biggest fool in the world."

Matt couldn't help grinning at that. "Isn't that better than being the second biggest?" he said. And Carter joined him in the laugh.

"I hope I'll learn someday, sir."

"Don't hope. Do it. Hoping is a luxury out here."

"Yes, I'm beginning to see that, sir."

"A man has to be hard out here, you know; but at the same time he has to be resilient."

"It's what my wife is always telling me," Carter said. "That I'm too stiff, too rigid, too demanding of myself and of others."

It was then that Matt Kincaid had a crazy thought, and before he knew what he was saying, the words popped out. "Sometimes when a man's like that," he said, "it makes other people who are close to him feel lonesome." He had been thinking of Edwina Carter, and the glance she had cast in his direction one evening just after dinner at the Conways. Matt had not acknowledged it, and she had looked away quickly, but there was no mistaking its meaning . . .

"Let's mount up, Mr. Carter," he said, turning and walking back toward his horse.

twelve ───────────

At the very moment that Matt Kincaid was thinking about her, Edwina Carter was sitting naked on the
edge of her bed, looking down at the young man lying
on his back—also naked—with his eyes closed. And
she was suddenly finding herself in the grip of a strange
and dreadful feeling. For the first time since she had
claimed she could tell the twins apart, she was not sure.
And while her mind told her she was imagining things,
there was still something tugging at her, some intuition
that somehow, something was different from the day
before when Will—it *was* Will?—had placed his head
in her lap and they had shortly afterward gone to bed
together. But today, though it had been equally passion-
ate, there had yet been something different that she was
not able to name.

It had been quite easy to tell Will from Walt the
afternoon of Flora Conway's tea party. And of course
she'd had to insist on not giving her "secret" away. But

the bulging rigidity in Will's trousers had been an easy giveaway. Only now, today, was Will still Will?

As the young man lying beside her opened his eyes, Edwina decided she would try something.

"Dear Walt, how are you feeling after your little nap?"

"The name is Will, Edwina. I guess it really isn't so easy to tell us apart."

"Oh. I guess not," Edwina said, her face suffused with a smile. She felt a sudden and tremendous relief to discover that she'd been wrong. Of course, it was always different with a man like this, wasn't it? It was with Dennis, certainly.

"Would you like a cup of tea, Will?"

"Yes, dear, kind, sweet, and most beautiful lady, I would love a cup of tea. And a kiss, please."

Edwina leaned down to attend to his second request, and she did not rise again for some time. By then it was too late for tea, and Will had only just departed when there came a knock at her door and Flora Conway's voice with an invitation to join herself and the captain for supper.

"Oh, I'd be very happy to," Edwina said, opening the door just enough to speak through. "I was just about to take a bath, but you could come in if you've a moment."

"I won't disturb you now, Edwina. We can talk later." And Flora was gone.

Edwina wondered if she had seen Will. But then she told herself that Will could easily have been bringing her hot water from the kitchen for her bath, which in fact was one of the details assigned the twins by Sergeant Cohen.

Flora Conway, crossing the parade in the late afternoon, also had her thoughts on the twins, wondering why Warner had been so adamant against inviting them to dinner that evening with Edwina Carter. Although most of the time she was able to win her husband over on

130

social matters, there were times when Warner could simply not be moved. This was such a time.

A short while later, when she was back in her quarters taking a bath, she was surprised to hear the door open and Warner calling her name.

"I'm in here, Warner. My, what are you doing off duty at such an early hour?" And she beamed up at him from the tub in which she lay soaking.

"Thought I'd drop over just to give your back a scrub."

"Oh, how wonderful!" And she bent down toward her knees, exposing her long white back and shoulders.

But it wasn't her back that her husband really had in mind, as she discovered the moment he slipped his hands around to fondle her breasts.

"Warner, dear, what are you doing!"

"I'm not taking morning roll call, Flora. Now, will you kindly step out of that tub?"

"But . . . while you're still on duty, dear?" She had turned her head, her long black hair spilling down over her breasts as her eyes mocked him gently.

"Flora, do I have to give you a direct order!"

"I just can't understand what's come over you, Warner. Have you been drinking?" But she was swiftly out of the tub, drying herself with her towel and moving toward the bed.

Warner Conway didn't answer. He was already pulling off his clothes, and now she was helping him, delighted to find him so relaxed from his usual military rigidity.

Later, as they both began to dress, she asked him, "Warner, do the twins take care of the Carter quarters? I mean, do they do any work for Edwina?"

"I believe so. I believe Ben Cohen has assigned them that detail once or twice. Why do you ask, dear?"

"No reason. I just thought it might be nice for Edwina if she had some help."

"I'll check it with Cohen." He had been fussing with the buttons on his balbriggans, and now he stopped and stood looking at her. "What have you got on your mind, Flora?"

His wife sighed. "I don't know that I can really say. It's... well, I have a rather strong feeling that Carter and Edwina are... having difficulties."

"I see."

"And I also wondered why you didn't want to have the boys to dinner tonight."

Warner Conway buttoned the last button on his uniform. "I think, my dear, it's because there's something about those two that I don't trust." He moved toward her and kissed her on the cheek, then walked into the other room.

Flora, who had been brushing her hair in front of her mirror, put down her brush and looked at herself. She was suddenly caught in surprise at the worried frown she saw there.

She was standing there wearing only a cotton shift, looking at herself in the mirror, when Warner came back into the room.

"I hear some commotion outside," he said. "Sounds like Kincaid and the patrol might be back."

Just at that moment there came a knocking at the door.

They were fifty—lean and muscular, bronzed and naked to the waist, their faces without expressions—the young Hunkpapas of Long Horse's band. They sat their ponies or stood, holding their rifles. Most of them were armed with the new Spencer repeating rifle, treasured weapon taken during the Battle of the Little Big Horn and at other bloody encounters with the whites. The rest were carrying single-shot Springfields, and some even had quivers hanging from their eager bodies, holding the red-striped arrows of the Sioux warrior. Their faces were painted red. They were ready, waiting stoically as Fox and Two Coyotes, seated on buffalo robes, conferred with Long Horse.

"Fifty Hunkpapa," Fox was saying. "And we, the Oglalla, make more." He did not specify the number of Oglalla braves, for they were fewer: only thirty.

Long Horse was a tall man, not yet twenty-five, proud to be a Hunkpapa, a member of Sitting Bull's tribe.

"It is good," Two Coyotes said. "Together we can whip the bluelegs."

"I had news of the fight at the Greybull," said Long Horse.

"It was but a skirmish," Fox replied aggressively. "We wished to try their strength. It is the little fort that we wish to burn to the ground."

They had smoked, the three young leaders, and now they planned the extermination of Outpost Number Nine.

"They have only Springfields," Two Coyotes said. "Many of the Oglalla and Hunkpapa now have the fast-talking gun."

"Spencer."

"Yes. Spencer is quicker."

"How many are at the little fort?"

"A company."

"Three platoons," said Long Horse, who, like any good Sioux leader, was wholly familiar with army organization.

"Once we rub out the American fort, other Lakotas will come to fight with us." Two Coyotes moved his hand several times as he spoke, indicating that many, many warriors would join them.

"Our young men are ready, eager for battle," Fox said. "We know that the Americans can be defeated by a clever attack."

"You do not have Crazy Horse now," Long Horse pointed out.

133

"You do not have Sitting Bull or Gall," replied Two Coyotes, referring to the Hunkpapa leaders who had been at the Little Big Horn with Crazy Horse, the Oglalla, for the big rubout of the whites.

Long Horse nodded. "No, we do not have any of the great ones now."

"But we have ourselves," Fox said boldly, a frown on his face.

Long Horse's piercing eyes surveyed the two Oglallas. It was a question of who would be chief in the coming battle. He did not wish to get embroiled in arguing about it. For him, rubbing out the whites was the main point. But he could see that Fox, the Oglalla, wanted to be leader. He realized that Two Coyotes was a man of caution and good sense, not crazy for power. He knew them both; he had no illusions about the proposed alliance. He knew how Owl Feather felt about fighting the whites: the same as the old Hunkpapa chief, Medicine Horn. Old men—wise, yes, but they had given up. It was up to the young to carry the battle now, before it became too late. Look at the Greasy Grass battle, what the whites called the Little Big Horn; the tribes had gained a smashing victory. And yet the Old Ones were saying that the war with the whites was all over. It was a lie. Yes, in this he shared conviction with these two Oglallas.

Now he picked up a stick near the buffalo robe on which he was sitting, and handed it to Two Coyotes. "Show the picture of the fort."

Leaning forward, Two Coyotes drew in the dirt a map of Outpost Number Nine and its approaches.

"There is one gate," he said.

"A gate that we could strike with one of the Singing Wire poles and with fire arrows," Fox said.

But Long Horse said, "We will lose too many warriors that way."

Fox allowed himself a smile as he swelled to the

134

moment. "That is why we have a plan."

"A plan?"

"Yes." He looked at Two Coyotes, fearful that he might speak ahead of him, but his friend was content to remain silent. "We have two allies inside the fort."

"Ah!" Long Horse was clearly interested. He had been a little suspicious of meeting with the two Oglallas before. He could see the sense in joining forces to fight the hated Americans—which was what the Sioux called the white soldiers, with no awareness of the bitter irony that the name implied—but he was still wary of Fox because of his violent wish for power. But now, if there were allies within the white man's fort—ah, that was another matter.

"Who is there?" Long Horse asked. "You have warriors inside the white fort? How is that?"

"Not warriors," Fox explained. "White men."

"Whites!"

"Two whites," Fox said, with his eyes on Two Coyotes. And now he turned directly to Long Horse. "Two magical whites."

"Ah—whites with special medicine? How can that be? I have never heard of a white man with medicine."

Two Coyotes held out his hands, with the palms up. "These are not men. They are boys. They are Look-Likes."

"They will do what we wish," Fox said. "We have but to signal them."

135

thirteen ───────────

Dutch Rothausen and his cooks outdid themselves. It was a dinner that would be remembered at Outpost Number Nine, albeit not without the memory of the stiff body of Private Mark Fitzhugh being lowered into the ground and Captain Warner Conway reading the burial service, and Privates Holzer and Malone filling the grave, and the whole of Easy Company standing at attention as Reb McBride blew taps.

But now it was evening, and in the officers' mess the CO, his adjutant, and his three platoon leaders, plus Flora Conway and Edwina Carter, were dining. Roast chicken and boiled potatoes a la Rothausen—that is, smothered in thick though well-seasoned gravy—formed the axis of the meal. It was a meal shared by the men of First Platoon in their own messhall. One marked difference was the presence of wine at the officers' banquet, courtesy of the post commander.

Matt Kincaid actually had not been in the mood for

any sort of celebration, feeling tired and somber from the events of the past few days; but Conway had reminded him that it was a famous man's birthday.

"I am rather dashed that you have forgotten, Lieutenant Kincaid," Conway said now in a voice jovial from the anticipation of wine.

"But whose birthday, Warner?" Flora asked. "What famous person?"

Matt looked over at the captain and his lady, seated at the head of the table. They certainly made a nice-looking couple, he decided, then his eyes swept to Carter and his wife. They did too, he thought, except for something in both their expressions—a sort of querulousness.

But the captain was raising his glass, and Lieutenants Fletcher and Williams, commanding Second and Third Platoons, had followed suit.

"Whoever it is, I'll drink to him—or her," Fletcher added quickly, and tried to hide his confusion as he looked at Flora Conway. He was a sandy-haired man with hazel eyes and a waxed mustache.

"Who can it be, sir?" asked Williams, seated beside Fletcher. "I know it isn't me!" And a ripple of laughter circled the table.

"Somebody very famous, talented, handsome, intelligent, virtuous—well, maybe not all that virtuous..." And more laughter followed this.

"Warner, will you please tell us who you are talking about? I'm dying to drink my wine," said Flora.

Matt had roused himself now, and began to feel more a part of things. "Are we supposed to guess, sir?"

"Oh, yes," said Edwina Carter, clapping her hands together. "A man? A woman? Let me see..." And she squinted her eyes, looking extraordinarily attractive, Kincaid thought.

"All right, all right," Conway said, raising his glass. "I can see you're all impatient to get to the liquid that

138

supports this meal." Holding his glass high, he looked around the table as the others raised their wine in readiness for the toast.

Edwina was beaming at Dennis Carter; he could feel her thigh pressing his beneath the table. At the same time, his face was flushed and he kept his eyes on his wineglass until Edwina nudged him.

"Darling..."

With a start, Carter raised his head, and looked at Captain Conway.

Conway was smiling. "I see that the mystery is becoming unbearable, so I'll simply say—and I know I can speak for all of us—a very, very happy birthday to our own, let me say, our one and only Matthew Kincaid!"

"My God!" Matt exclaimed. "I...I completely forgot, sir."

"I know you forgot, but today's the day!" Conway beamed on his second-in-command and handed him a small package. "I wish it were your captain's bars, but maybe you'll enjoy this better."

"Indeed I will, sir," Matt said as he unwrapped the package, revealing a box of cigars.

Amid much laughter, the group settled down to the meal.

Flora suddenly looked over at Edwina Carter. "Why, what's the matter, dear?"

Edwina shook her head, wiping her eyes. "I was laughing," she said, and she reached over and squeezed her husband's hand. "Sometimes when I laugh I even cry."

Flora saw the deep flush on Dennis Carter's face and wondered what could be wrong. But the moment passed. Warner Conway had started to tell them a story.

Matt, sniffing the open box of cigars, had been only half listening, with his thoughts on how he was going to enjoy his present.

Now Conway's words began to cut in on his attention. "You could've knocked me over with a feather, I was that surprised to see him. Of course, I'd no idea who he was when he rode in."

"The man who was here the day before yesterday, Warner?" Flora asked.

"Oh," said Edwina. "That man with the beard and wearing so many clothes?"

This brought a laugh from the group. "Those old-timers like to dress warm even in summer," Williams said. "I was surprised too, sir. He's really a quiet sort."

"Who?" Matt asked. "I didn't catch the name."

"Phillips," Conway said. "Portugee John Phillips."

"He was here?"

"Stopped over on his way to Laramie. Didn't stay. Just wanted to grain his horse and set one of his shoes."

"That was a bit of a different ride than the one he made from Phil Kearny, I'll wager," Fletcher said. "We all heard about that back at the Point."

"Oh, *that* man!" Lieutenant Carter was nodding vigorously. "Sir, is that the man who rode all those miles to Laramie when Red Cloud was attacking the fort up on the Bozeman Trail?"

"The very same," Conway said. "And you know, he's not such an old man. About my age, I'd guess."

"What's he doing now?" Matt asked.

"Ranching near Glenrock, he said. I don't know what he was doing around here, but I was glad to see him. Tried to get him to stay over. But no." He snorted suddenly. "You and me—we all complain about late pay. You know Portugee never got a cent for what he did? Not even a medal." The Captain's face showed his disgust.

"My God!" said Carter. "That really is not fair, sir! I find it hard to believe that the government would treat such a man that way."

"But what happened?" Edwina asked.

And Flora echoed her. "What happened to this man Phillips?"

"Oh, everyone knows the story," Conway said. "Well, no; ladies, I apologize." He reached for his glass and took a generous swallow of wine. "It was in '66, when Red Cloud and the Sioux were really about to wipe out Phil Kearny."

"Is that a town?" Edwina asked.

"A fort on the Bozeman Trail," Matt told her.

"Colonel Henry Carrington commanding," Carter added.

Conway cleared his throat, marshaling his facts before speaking. "Red Cloud was one tough fellow. You know, Washington made peace with him finally, and Washington had to sign the peace *his* way. It's the only time the Indians ever did have it their way."

"But—" Carter started to object, but then stopped abruptly, casting his eyes down.

By God, thought Kincaid, maybe the kid's beginning to learn.

"Anyway," Conway was saying, "the Sioux had Kearny surrounded, with Red Cloud simply waiting for the big freeze to set in before he'd move in and wipe them out. You all know of the Fetterman Massacre, when he lured some 80 men of the 18th Infantry into a trap outside the fort, and slaughtered the lot. An example of recklessness, I might add for the benefit of our younger officers, by the leader of the troops, Captain William J. Fetterman, who had bragged how with eighty men he could ride through the entire Sioux nation. But he didn't figure on the architect of his disaster—Crazy Horse. Matt, you tell it. I'm dry in the whistle."

Matt had been watching Carter to see how he was taking Conway's comments on Fetterman, whom he had tried praising to Matt. But Carter's face was without expression. Maybe, Matt thought, just maybe . . .

Now he grinned, putting down his glass. "That's the background. The fort was in a panic; about a hundred soldiers and civilians were there to greet the bodies of the victims. You can imagine, it was no party. They figured Red Cloud would attack the fort itself, and pretty soon."

"How many Indians were there?" Edwina asked.

"The estimate was about three thousand."

A whisper of awe went up from the dinner table.

"Now the nearest telegraph station was 197 miles away, and reinforcements were 237 miles. I believe those are the correct figures." He looked at Conway, who nodded.

"So what did they do?" Edwina asked. "What happened?"

"Well, the temperature was way down. It was snowing. So who would ride through three thousand Sioux and all those miles in subzero weather in the hope of getting help?"

"Portugee what's-his-name," said Flora.

"Right. Phillips was a civilian handyman on the post, and he volunteered to Carrington to take a message to Laramie if the colonel would lend him his own horse. The horse happened to be a thoroughbred."

Matt looked over at Conway. "So that's it."

"He did it?" Edwina's eyes were sparkling with excitement.

"He did it." Conway put down his glass. "He rode through the storm and the Sioux, carrying some pieces of hardtack for himself and some grain for his horse. He was shot at and chased by the Sioux, he nearly froze to death, but he reached Laramie at eleven o'clock on Christmas night. He only just made it, I mean physically."

142

"And his horse, sir?" asked Carter, and Matt looked at him quickly.

"His horse died," Conway said. "But Fort Phil Kearny was saved. Troops left Laramie the following morning and got there in time. Red Cloud couldn't attack, and the ending was happy. Of course, later the Bozeman was closed, according to Red Cloud's treaty terms with the whites."

A silence fell on the group now, as Conway concluded his story.

After a moment Matt said, "What has happened to our guests, Captain?"

"Our twins are still with us, and I've wired again to Regiment. Sergeant Cohen and the entire post, in fact, have had their hands full. But I don't think that surprises you. Their story of how and why they got out here is still suspicious, and especially after hearing from Edwina that they showed quite a bit of hatred toward the army. Which in itself isn't anything so terrible; it's only that I personally still feel uncomfortable about them."

"But they're just boys," Flora said, coming in right away. "You know, young people are very impressionable. And bear in mind that they've been through a terrible time. It must have been sheer horror in Georgia."

"I do agree with you," Edwina said. "Oh, yes, they've had a fearful experience. And with the Indians too."

Matt saw the scowl on Carter's face as he said, "My dear, we cannot afford to behave like a bleeding-heart society when we have rebels in our midst."

His wife dropped her eyes, her cheeks flushing. Yet Carter was only just starting. "I think they're a couple of brats who should be disciplined. Edwina, I'm ashamed of you for even thinking in that manner!"

Conway was already clearing his throat. "In any case, I'm sure we'll have news shortly from Regiment."

143

The dinner ended shortly after that. It wasn't late, but everyone was tired. Matt was the last guest to leave, and Conway suggested a smoke and a glass of the brandy he kept for special occasions. Matt, tired as he was, was delighted as he took a seat.

They had been going over the patrol's tour in the field again, but in a much more relaxed manner, and had once again discussed the Kenning boys, when Flora came back into the room, grimacing at the dense cigar smoke.

"Did either of you gentlemen wonder what was going on with the Carters when we all toasted Matt's birthday?"

"As a matter of fact, yes," said her husband. "What the devil was that all about? She definitely started to cry, and he looked like he'd swallowed a live rattlesnake."

Flora sat down on the horsehair sofa, her knees together with her hands crossed on top of them. "It wasn't so funny," she said. "This is an incredible coincidence, and it couldn't have happened to a more sensitive person—but it isn't only Matt Kincaid's birthday. It's also Dennis Carter's."

The truly desperate time for Sergeant Ben Cohen began when the message came clicking over the telegraph wire from Regiment.

The company clerk winced at the outraged bellow and the string of curses that followed.

"Wouldn't you know! Just wouldn't you know!" Cohen was purple as he strode up and down the orderly room. "Regiment doesn't have any room for the little darlin's, and suggests—get that, Corporal Bradshaw— *suggests* that we continue to hold them while we contact St. Joe, Atlanta, and Washington, D.C., or just dump the dear boys out into the big bad world! Holy Mother of God!"

"Gee, Sarge—"

"You've heard the latest, Bradshaw, have you?" The

144

sergeant stood bristling in front of the company clerk's desk.

"What's that, Sarge?" Four Eyes was afraid his glasses would fog up under the rage of Easy Company's first sergeant.

"You've not heard? Well, it's French monte they're playing, and skinning not only the company, but the civilians to boot. And they've gotten real open about it. Given up the show of being sweet little innocents that they started out with—when was it? Five days, six days ago? It feels like a year!"

Bradshaw was about to speak, but the sergeant was glaring at him and he began to fear that what he had to say would be the cause of a further uproar and possibly even physical violence. But Four Eyes had courage that sometimes transcended his fear, and this was one of those times.

"Sarge, do you think those boys are cheating?"

Ben Cohen had been pacing the room, and now he stopped as though thunderstruck. He stood—planted like a monolith—directly in front of his clerk's desk, his eyes bulging, his thick neck red.

"Cheating? For Christ's sake, where the hell are your eyes, Corporal!" Then he added, "Your glasses must need cleaning. Cheating? Shit, they've slickered every man in this here company."

He paused, sucking in air, his jaws working, his face and neck aflame. "But listen to me, Bradshaw. We are going to scissor those two little bastards. What I need is evidence."

Four Eyes began to feel funny all over as the Sergeant surveyed him carefully, rocking back and forth just a little bit on his heels. He was afraid he knew what was coming.

"I have got a plan."

"Yes, Sarge."

"Here's what I want you to do."

"Sure, Sarge." Four Eyes had to force some strength into his voice.

"First, go get Malone."

The game started to pick up when Malone covered a couple of Will Kenning's large bets—large by army pay standards—losing one and winning the other. When Will passed the dice, Malone came out on a nine, and offered to borrow on the six-ace draw for three dollars.

"On nines and fives I bet on the make," Will said firmly. Gone was the innocent approach the boys had started off with when they came to the post five days earlier. Of the two, Will had been especially impatient with the lack of money at Easy Company, and had totally given up any pretense at being a fledgling gambler. In fact, the new role both boys had adopted proved to be more agreeable to the men of Outpost Number Nine, some of whom were eager to learn the craft so ably practiced by the twins, and all of whom were overawed by it. In their new image, the boys had given out that their wealthy Uncle Milford, who owned a number of plantations, had loved to gamble—like all Southern gentlemen—and had often entertained them by teaching them what he knew of the gaming tables.

"I'll make it for three dollars," Malone said cautiously.

"Make it five," Will said, shoving in the money.

Malone—not worrying too much, for it was the sergeant's money—called almost simultaneously as he cast the dice.

Without even glancing down at the dice, Will reached out and caught them, and as he hurled them back to Malone, he said, "A dollar more you don't make it." While Four Eyes, standing right beside him, swallowed several times, his Adam's apple pumping up and down furiously.

Malone was sweating, for he was dying to let go and swing into the spirit of the game; but at the same time he was concerned that he and Four Eyes should carry out Sergeant Ben Cohen's explicit instructions. He counted out the money and bumped the dice hard against the wall. They spun around before settling down right in the middle of a floor plank. The throw was a six-ace, and a muted roar went up from the onlookers. For a moment Malone forgot it was the sergeant's money and turned white, thinking he had lost half a month's pay on a single throw:

"I think them dice are crooked, by God," he spat out and reached for them.

"That is not true," Will said, grabbing Malone's wrist.

In that second, Bradshaw moved, knocking into Will, and at the same time striking his other hand.

In a moment the room was in an uproar, and Malone was in his glory, trading punches with both twins. It took no time at all for the whole group to get into it.

Later, when Four Eyes walked into the orderly room, Ben Cohen said, "Did you get 'em?"

Four Eyes held out his fist and slowly opened it in front of Cohen. The Sergeant took the dice, shook them in his own hand, and tossed them onto his desk.

"Nine," he said.

He threw again. "Six."

And then he threw a five. Picking them up, he examined them closely.

"What do you see, Sarge?" Four Eyes asked.

"These the ones he was shooting with?"

"They're the ones he palmed," Four Eyes said. "He's very fast."

"Quicker'n a cat lickin' his ass," Malone said, walking into the orderly room. "Is it what you wanted, Sarge?"

Cohen surveyed Private Malone with a glint in his eye. "It is." Now he grinned. "You didn't have much trouble, I see. A few scratches, maybe a bruise here or there."

"Malone takes good care of Malone, Sergeant."

"That I know."

The sergeant threw the dice on the desk again. An eight. Then another eight, a nine, a three, and a six.

"It never throws seven?" asked Four Eyes.

"Not the six-ace, and that's how you were betting."

"The sons of bitches have been throwing tops all along," said Malone.

"That is correct, Private Malone. You didn't have the chance of a fart in a windstorm, going up against that feller." The look on the first sergeant's face was grim. "And the money, Malone. Did you get the money back?"

"Ah, yes, Sarge. I got it." And Malone apologetically fished into his pants pocket and withdrew the sergeant's money.

"Good," said Sergeant Cohen.

"Any time, Sergeant Cohen," Malone said.

And with a wink at Bradshaw, Private Malone turned on his heel and walked out of the orderly room.

Cohen picked up the dice.

"The other dice was just regular dice, that it, Sarge?" Four Eyes asked.

"Right. They're flats. All you gotta do is switch 'em. Did you see him switch, Bradshaw?"

Four Eyes hesitated. Then he said slowly, "To be honest, Sarge, no. I couldn't see it. But I know he did it."

"So do I," Ben Cohen said. "So do I."

fourteen _____

In spite of himself, Matt Kincaid was finding a certain sympathy for young Dennis Carter. Yes, the man was a fool, he was arrogant, but there was something else about him, a youthful eagerness and naivete, that was appealing. It was as though what he really felt had been covered over, and he was not free to just be himself. Matt remembered the time he had commented on the beautiful country out on patrol; and he had noticed him a few other times, looking at some of the scenery as though he felt something about it. And yet he spoke to his wife badly in public, and he was filled with a virulent hatred for the Indian.

Later, after leaving Captain Conway following the birthday dinner, Matt found he wasn't as sleepy as he had thought, and so he decided to take a walk around the post. He wanted to think. He was pretty sure that by now Fox and Two Coyotes had hooked up with Long Horse, but he hadn't yet heard from Windy Mandalian.

The scout had been gone since the day before, and Matt was looking for him anytime now, bringing news of the situation.

He had just passed the stables. He heard a horse nicker in its stall and saw a figure standing at the corner of the building.

"Oh—" The startled voice was that of a woman.

"Excuse me," Matt said. And then he saw who it was. "Mrs. Carter, I'm sorry if I frightened you."

"Oh, no, I'm quite all right, Lieutenant. I was just taking the air."

The moon was up and it wasn't totally dark, but he couldn't see her face to verify what her voice told him— that she had been crying.

Without noticing it, they had started to walk slowly together across the parade. After a moment he felt her movement beside him as she took out a handkerchief.

"Are you all right, ma'am?"

"Yes. Yes, I think so."

"If I can be of any help..."

Another long pause fell, and finally she said, "It's Dennis. Would there be any chance of our getting a transfer, Lieutenant?"

"Why? Can you tell me what's wrong? I mean, you've barely just gotten here."

After a moment she said, speaking very softly, "There's nothing really wrong. Not in the usual way. It's that...it's just that Dennis is so bent on this thing about the Indians. That's what he talks about all the time. I imagine you've heard him."

"Yes, I have. But what is it?"

"He is not happy. I mean, with me." And now she bent her head to her handkerchief and he saw that she was crying.

"Lots of married people have their troubles, Mrs. Carter." Matt said.

"He is so terribly, terribly jealous."

"A lot of men suffer from that, you know. And you, ma'am, if I may say so, are a beautiful woman."

"But he is jealous of everyone. Even . . . even of those two young boys. Oh, it's so awful! You know, I was so happy to have him back here safe and sound, and he's hardly spoken to me or . . . or anything else. You heard him at dinner. He's so often angry."

They had stopped walking now, and were standing close together under the eave of a building. It was quite dark; he could barely see her outline. But he could feel her closeness.

Suddenly she was in his arms, their bodies pressed close together, and he could feel the trembling going through both of them as his mouth found hers.

"Oh, Matt . . . Matt . . ."

A horse whinnied somewhere and Matt stepped back.

"Forgive me, ma'am, but I—"

"Oh, no, oh, no . . . it's beautiful." And she reached out and touched his arm.

"It is indeed beautiful, Edwina, but it isn't wise. It had best stop now before it gets started."

She was silent for a long moment, then she said, "Yes. I know you're right."

When he walked into the officers' barracks he found Mr. Carter waiting for him.

It was a moment Kincaid did not savor. And while he stood facing Carter, he tried to figure out what he would say. But his suspicion was unfounded.

"Sir, if you have a few moments, there is something I feel the need to talk to you about."

"Come in," Kincaid said, and preceded him into the dayroom. "Have a seat."

"It's about the Indians, sir."

"What about them?"

"I *want* to understand, sir. I really do. But I find it difficult."

"I told you it wasn't easy out here, Mr. Carter. It's a whole different world. There isn't anything like it anywhere, I'm sure of that."

"What I find so difficult, sir, is this attitude toward the Indians. I mean, they try to kill us. Oh, I know there are some peaceful ones. Maybe a lot. But the ones who aren't, like Fox and Two Coyotes... well, I just don't understand the army's attitude, or—forgive me sir, and with all respect—your attitude and Captain Conway's."

"What is my attitude, Lieutenant?" Matt asked. "Maybe if you tell me what you think it is, it might help clear things a little."

Carter was having a difficult time. He looked down at his hands, then across at the opposite wall. "It just seems to me that if someone's an avowed enemy, then you go all-out to kill him, wipe him out. I mean you—"

"Exterminate him?" Matt said.

"Exactly, sir. That's just what I mean. But here we make no effort to carry the war to its conclusion. There are skirmishes, little campaigns and a battle here and there... but why not a large scale attack on these tribes around us who are continually *asking* to be whipped?"

"In other words, you mean why do we do everything so cautiously?"

"Well, I guess you could put it that way, sir."

"Right. I can't say I disagree with you. Because to you, it all seems like a sort of game. Isn't that it?"

"That's it, sir. That's it." Carter nodded his head and shrugged. "I just don't understand it."

Kincaid fell silent for a long moment, and the two of them sat there in the large empty room. When his superior officer still said nothing, Carter began to feel uneasy. Still, he controlled himself, keeping the silence. Finally

152

it became unbearable and he finally spoke.

"I'm sorry, sir. I guess I have spoken out of turn again."

But now Kincaid turned to him. "It's difficult to answer your question, Mr. Carter. You see, I look at it this way . . . we don't want to kill Indians. Of course, there are a great many people who do, mind you. But I don't, Captain Conway doesn't, Windy doesn't. We want them to honor their treaties. I think that's it. At the same time, I for one can understand why they don't. I likely wouldn't myself, if I were a Sioux or a Cheyenne or Arapaho." He paused, looking at the backs of his fingers as he held his hand in front of him.

"But I'm a white man. I'm a soldier in the United States Army, and I agreed to perform what we call our duty. That duty is to maintain the peace. The government has decreed that the Indian should live on the land allotted to him by treaty. And to maintain the peace, we have been put here, in part, to see that he does that. A lot of Indians agree with that, and are willing to abide by the treaties they have signed. Some, unfortunately, aren't. Then we have problems. Our biggest difficulty is in treading that fine line between seeing that the Indians obey the law and in remembering that they are human beings."

Matt stood up and stretched, and Carter stood up also; for once he seemed to have no reply to Matt's statements.

Kincaid looked at the younger officer and said, perhaps a bit sadly, "Of course, Mr. Carter, we will win. We're the future. Some Indians, like Owl Feather, know that and are willing to bend. Others, though they may know in deep in their hearts, will fight us. And they will suffer for it, and many brave men on both sides will die."

"Hear me, my brothers! It is true that many of our Lakota are beaten and enslaved by the *Wasichu*, the whites. But we are not!" It was Fox speaking, standing tall before

153

the many braves, his voice firm, confident, and angry.

"We have seen our people coming as beggars to the whites to be fed scraps by their master!"

A chorus of sullen agreement with Fox's words rose from the listeners. He looked across the small campfire at the foot of the cliff. To his left stood Two Coyotes, and to his right, Long Horse. Day was breaking and the three leaders had called the warriors to hear the words before their final march to wipe out Outpost Number Nine.

"Now we will avenge our people, and free them. It is we who will rub out the *Wasichu* and show everyone the way back to the Shining Times. And once again all will be good, and the game plentiful!"

A loud murmur of approval greeted the conclusion of Fox's speech. Now the Oglallas and Hunkpapas prepared for the final stage of their journey, checking their horses, their weapons, and the honored paint on their hard young bodies.

The three leaders now retreated to the edge of the creek, where they sat and smoked and conferred on their final plans.

"Everything will depend on the Look-Likes, then," said Long Horse.

"Not everything," Two Coyotes pointed out. "Much, to be sure, will depend on them, but the final blow will be ours."

"It is so," Long Horse agreed. "Only it is necessary to get inside the little fort."

"The signal," Fox said, "will be sent. Full Moon will take it."

"Can we be sure of the Look-Likes?" Long Horse now asked. "They may be magical, and maybe not. I am not sure. Their whiteness may be only an American white-ness."

Fox nodded at the careful observation. "It is wise to

be cautious," he said. "The two hate the Americans. Two Coyotes and I have heard them. They were in the big war when the bluelegs fought one another. They spoke of this while they were with us. It is why they came to us, they said, even though we captured them."

"And you let them escape to the Americans' little fort." Long Horse spoke with his eyes half closed, following his thoughts.

"They will help us," Fox said, and he felt annoyed that the Hunkpapa was questioning his decision. "That has been our agreement."

"It is good, then," Long Horse said, opening his eyes more and looking at Fox. "But we need to be sure."

"It is certain. Of course, there is always a chance that something is not foreseen."

Two Coyotes had fallen silent. The three men were sitting in a semicircle, facing the creek. Above them the sun rose toward the top of the sky. It glinted on the purling creek water, its heat strengthening the smell of their horses, the buffalo grass, the sage.

After several moments had passed, Long Horse said, "Two Coyotes is silent."

Fox, sensing some criticism from his friend, stirred uneasily, ready to argue.

For another moment or so, no one said anything, and then Two Coyotes spoke.

"My thoughts are on the bluelegs and on the Look-Likes. What you say, Long Horse, is true. And so what is needed is a second plan. So that all will be certain."

"A second plan." The scowl took up the whole of Fox's face.

Long Horse's eyes narrowed slightly. "What is your plan?" he asked.

Two Coyotes looked up at the sky. A flock of chickadees swooped down close to where they sat, but he was watching a lone eagle soaring, far away.

"We can take a lesson," he said slowly. "You remember the fight at the fort on the trail the Americans call Bozeman?"

"Ah . . . the fight when Crazy Horse rubbed out all the *Wasichu*."

"It worked for the one the Oglallas called the Strange Man," Two Coyotes said. "It could work for us."

fifteen _____

At Outpost Number Nine the men had finished supper, but now, instead of their usual routine, they were following orders from Conway and Kincaid and cleaning their rifles and handguns, checking their ammunition, and preparing for whatever emergency might appear. Kincaid had assigned extra men to guard duty. He had also spoken with Dutch Rothausen about preparing his casualty detail, and had told Olsen that he wanted half a squad assigned to blanket detail to smother any fires before they got out of hand. Windy Mandalian was still out trying to locate some sign of the hostiles.

"Of course, sir," Matt said to Conway, "they might not be planning to attack here at all." They were standing on the eastern wall, looking out over the long sweep of prairie.

"But you suspect they might, from the way Owl Feather was talking."

"Both Windy and I think they will attack, sir. I'm

only allowing for the other possibility. That is, that they might hit some of the surrounding civilians first."

"You've sent messengers to warn the homesteaders?"

"Yes, sir. That's all taken care of."

"Then we'll simply have to wait. Windy will have news." Conway studied his adjutant for a moment, and then said, "I have the definite feeling, Lieutenant Kincaid, that you are still not satisfied with what took place last week."

"There was something not right about that little skirmish, sir. Those boys got away from Mr. Lo too easily."

"I agree," Conway said, nodding. "I agree. But what have we learned since they've been here? Not much. They're not telling the whole truth. They've been taking the men at cards and dice like hallelujah. And they've been graying the hair of our first sergeant."

"And Regiment doesn't want 'em," said Matt with a sigh. "What are we going to do with them, Captain?"

"I'll talk to Regiment again. They've got to be sent back East or something, but that's Regiment's work, not ours. I mean, as I see it."

Matt had just left the captain and was checking the lookout tower when he saw the lone figure riding in on the blue roan. Man and horse came in a direct line to the gate, and as he slipped out of his saddle, Windy Mandalian handed Kincaid an arrow with three red stripes painted on it.

"Where's it from?" Matt asked as the scout led his horse into the stable.

"From the body of a man named Sol Bolling. Sodbuster up on the east fork of the Greybull. The warning got to him too late."

"Hell, are they heading this way, or just staying out to get some horses and coups?"

Windy swiftly stripped the roan and grained him, and now they began walking toward the mess hall. "I figure it's a decoy. We ride out after them to protect the homesteaders, and they hit the fort, besides chopping us to pieces. They all think they're Crazy Horse."

"Thank God they aren't."

"Some of them try pretty hard to be, Matt," Windy said as they walked into the mess hall and sat down.

The big room was empty, but there was supper still in the kitchen—beans and sourdough bread and coffee. Dutch Rothausen observed that the scout ate enough for three men.

"Keeps me growin'," Windy said with a wink at Matt, and added under his breath, "Shit, he acts like what he cooks is pure gold."

"That's what it is, by God!" Rothausen said, over-hearing. "Just please leave a little so some of us poor, humble cooks can keep up our strength too." And he thumped off on his heavy feet, scratching his belly as he disappeared into the kitchen.

"The rest of the outlying soddies and such are taken care of, then," Matt said.

"They're all right. They've grouped over at Hillman's, on the crossing at Wood River. I told 'em to come on in here, but they said no." He sniffed at the food. "They'll do fine. Hillman's a good man."

A step behind them announced the arrival of Captain Conway, who, before either of them could acknowledge his presence, slipped onto the bench alongside Matt, so that both officers were now facing Windy Mandalian.

"Well," said the captain. "Now that you can feed your private army, maybe you could tell us what's going on out there on the lonesome prairie."

Windy kept right on eating, his big jaws chomping on his food. Matt grinned; he knew Windy never took kindly to repeating himself. So he quickly filled in the captain.

"So they're heading for here," Conway said.

159

The scout nodded, sucking his teeth loudly as he felt around with his tongue for any morsels that may have gotten stuck. "That's the size of it." He reached for his cup of coffee. "That lonesome prairie, as you call it, ain't so lonesome. Plenty Hunkpapa, plenty Oglalla, all painted up."

"When do you figure they'll hit us?" Matt asked.

"Not sure. Might be they'll sashay around through the territory, knocking on the doors of some ranches and soddies. I left Joseph Hatchet out there to keep track of them. Thought I'd ride on in with what I had."

"So it is definitely Fox and Two Coyotes," Conway said.

"And Long Horse."

"And Long Horse." Matt nodded.

"There's three of them," Windy went on. "Close to a hundred warriors, and they're not packing flintlocks, mind you. I'd say about half of them have got Spencers."

Conway swore.

Windy washed a swallow of coffee around in his mouth and let it down his long, skinny throat, then sat back on the bench. Kincaid knew his next move, and he saw the fascination in Conway's face as he witnessed the dexterity with which the scout severed the precise amount of tobacco from the plug he'd taken from his pocket, and with one flowing movement flipped it into his mouth. For an instant both Matt and Conway wondered if he would slice his tongue. The whole operation was like a little dance, the finale being the return of knife and to-bacco plug, and the closing of jaws.

"The men will be sleeping in shifts," Matt said, and he looked closely at Windy. "Maybe you'd better get some sleep, my friend."

"Good notion, that." Windy stood up and stretched. "I'll just wander over to Tipi Town for a look-see."

"I don't mean that kind of sleep!"

Conway gave a hoot of laughter, and Windy's lined face slipped into an easy grin. "I know what you meant, Lieutenant Kincaid, sir. And I know what *I* mean." And with a throaty chuckle, the long, lonesome scout moved out of the mess hall.

Matt and Warner Conway continued to sit where they were, sharing the laugh that the little scene with Windy had brought. They both knew that the scout would be the first man available, should there be any call to action, no matter where he was sleeping.

"He really is an animal," Conway said suddenly. And when Kincaid raised his eyebrows in surprise, he said, "I mean, he has the good sense of an animal. He knows how to take care of himself."

"He knows his own measure," Matt said.

"That's it. It's a rare trait," Conway said. He stood up.

"Matt, I don't know about you, but sleep is certainly not on my mind."

"Nor mine, sir."

"Well then, we have occasionally sampled my cigars. What do you say we sample a couple of yours?"

"I've got two right here in my pocket, sir," Matt said as he followed his CO outside.

Following the fisticuffs at the Malone-Bradshaw dice game, First Sergeant Ben Cohen had moved the twins from the enlisted men's barracks to a room off the mess hall. His purpose was twofold: the boys would be less available to the men, many of whom were only too eager to gamble, and they would be closer to where he could keep an eye on them. Captain Conway had sent off another message to Regiment, requesting that they take the Kennings, but so far no reply had been forthcoming. Meanwhile, the post was preparing for the possibility of an Indian attack.

161

It was late in the evening now—the same evening on which Matt Kincaid's birthday had been celebrated. The boys were seated on their bunks in their new quarters, smoking two cheroots they had stolen from the mess sergeant's supply, which he kept hidden in the icehouse. Walt was practicing cuts and second-dealing, while Will was marking a new deck of cards he'd swiped out of the officers' dayroom.

"You know Cohen sent another message to Regiment," Will was saying, intent on his work as he spoke without looking up at his brother.

"I heard him talking to Four Eyes. He said they'd better come back with something this time."

"Meaning—if he and Conway keep pushing—we might find ourselves worse off than we are here. Because for sure the report that will be sent along with us will not be rosy. And I'll bet all the way on that one."

Walt grimaced at that. "We have got to get our asses out of here, my lad."

"Do you think your lady friend will blab?"

"Do you think *yours* will?"

They both chuckled.

Will looked over at his brother then. "Think she tumbled?"

"I don't give a shit if she did."

"Nor I. I just wondered. But the point is for her husband *not* to tumble."

"That man has got a rifle up his ass. He'd probably beat the shit out of her if he even suspected anything."

"I think so. He's that type—no question there."

"Anyhow, as long as we are here, we'd better play it slow now that he's back. This damned army post is about as private as a Fourth of July celebration."

Will looked at his brother. "There's something up, isn't there?"

"I feel it." Walt put down the cards he'd been working

with. "Think they're expecting trouble?"

"Like from our old friends?"

"I noticed Holzer carrying his rifle when he went to the latrine."

They fell silent.

"Will . . ."

"Uh-huh."

"What about our plan?"

"What about it?"

"Kind of stalled, isn't it?"

"Maybe they forgot."

"Maybe. They were going to send a signal. Wonder what the hell they had in mind." Walt shook his head and reached for his deck of cards.

"Well, we'll have to keep a lookout for it, that's all. Shit, we're not mind-readers."

A long silence fell over them now, as they returned to their cards.

Will cleared his throat. "Walt . . ."

"What say?"

"You still want to?"

"Still want to!" Walt exclaimed, putting down his cards and looking at his brother.

"I've been wondering," Will said.

"Goddammit, Will! Are you getting cold feet, for Christ's sake?"

"No. I just wondered what you were thinking." Will looked down at his cards, feeling his twin's angry glare on him.

Suddenly the door of the room was thrown open and Lieutenant Carter strode in.

"Mr. Car . . ." Will started to say, but his words were cut off by the riding whip Carter slashed across his face.

Carter turned instantly and brought the whip down on Walt. Meanwhile, Will, recovering, and with blood running down his face, charged. But Carter's fury gave him

163

speed. Sidestepping, he drove his heavy boot into Will's crotch. The boy fell writhing to the floor. Carter now smashed Walt again with the whip, pursuing him around the room, as the boy tried in vain to get away from the rain of blows. Finally he fell to his knees, his nose smashed and one ear severely cut and pouring blood.

"You filthy swine!" Carter stood over both of them now, his fury giving him unassailable strength. "You goddamn bastard shits!"

Will had vomited, and was now trying to pull himself up by holding on to a chair. Carter yanked the support away from him.

"You can be thankful I don't kill or castrate the both of you!" And he began whipping the two of them again, across their backs and buttocks and legs.

Finally the blows ceased, and the boys lay motionless at his feet.

At length, the glaze left Carter's eyes. He looked down at the twins now, focusing. His shoulders relaxed, his eyes filled, and sobbing uncontrollably, he turned and hurried from the room.

It was a long while before Walt spoke. "Do you . . . do you still want to change your mind, Will?"

His brother had pulled himself up onto his bunk. He lay back, his head on his pillow. He didn't answer Walt, for his head had encountered some hard object, and now he reached painfully under the pillow and pulled out a Colt Dragoon revolver.

"What're you doing with my gun, damn you!" Walt snapped out, but with difficulty, for his lips were split.

Will was studying the weapon in his hand. "It isn't your gun, Walt," he said. "It's mine." And he fell back on the pillow, letting the pistol fall to the floor.

"What the hell are you talking about! That Indian took yours, don't you remember!" Walt sat up on the edge of his bed.

"It's mine," Will insisted, speaking slowly and with

his eyes closed. "It's the one that son of a bitch Fox took from me. Take a look; there's my mark on the grip."

Walt reached down and picked the gun off the floor and examined it. "By jingo, it is. It *is* your gun. How the devil did it get here?" His voice was still labored, but there was new life in it as he continued to examine the weapon.

"Doesn't matter," Will said, raising himself on his elbows. "It's here. We have got the message, clear and simple." He sat up, letting his feet fall to the floor.

"Christ, I'll kill that son of a bitch." he said.

"Let's get moving," said Will. "Maybe we can kill them all."

Kincaid and Conway were reaching the end of their cigars, and the captain had just added a dividend to the brandy glasses. They were seated in Conway's quarters. For a short while Flora had kept them company, but discovering that Edwina Carter had forgotten to take a book she'd asked to borrow, Flora decided to take a walk over to the Carter quarters and drop it off.

The two men didn't notice how much time had passed since Flora left them, for they'd been deep in discussion.

"I think he might be softening a little, sir." Matt said. "A couple of things I've noticed. But it's a long haul."

"Well, he could try to be a little more considerate to his wife," Conway said, "or so it seems to me. I mean, at least in public."

Matt nodded in agreement. "He has some crazy ideas about what it means to be manly, sir. For instance, he told me he thinks women should be broken, just like horses. And he thinks we should simply exterminate every Indian in the whole of the country. He didn't appreciate it when I pointed out that the Indians don't *break* their horses, they gentle them. It's the whites who go in for breaking."

A heavy sigh pushed past Conway's lips. "You've got

your hands full, Matt. You and Olsen too, I guess."

"Olsen is one damned good sergeant, sir, and he has been helpful. I don't know much about Carter's background, only that he has an older brother that everybody idolizes, and he tries to be like him. His wife told me that, and oddly, Carter himself told me the same thing when we were out on patrol. He opened up a good bit and began to see things a bit differently, I think." Matt paused. "I feel he's got some good in him."

"I hope he can be relied on for a cool head when the hostiles hit us," Conway said. "We don't want him pulling a Fetterman at this stage of the game. That's what I'm afraid of."

Matt's cigar had gone out, and he took a moment to relight it. He had just drawn on it when there was a knock at the door.

"Sergeant Cohen, Captain." The first sergeant's thunderous voice pierced the door.

"Come," Conway called.

"The guard told me you were both here, sir," Cohen said, his eyes falling on Kincaid. "Lieutenant, your orders are carried out, sir."

Conway looked questioningly at Matt.

"The Gatling, Captain."

"Where have you placed it?"

"Right behind the gate, sir. The hostiles won't see it. I'm thinking that they'll try to draw us away from the gate by hitting strongly at the west wall; or else they'll try to get us to ride out after them and set an ambush."

"They all think they can repeat the Wagon Box Fight."

"It's their specialty. But if they hit the gate, we'll be ready."

"Sir . . ."

Conway turned to his first sergeant.

"Captain, there is still nothing from Regiment concerning those guests, sir."

"Damn!"

Cohen's face was glowering. "Captain, I just took a look in their new quarters back of the mess hall, and they're completely torn up. Looks like a grizzly got in and went berserk—bedclothes torn up, chairs broken. The little bastards weren't there, and I haven't been able to find them."

Captain Conway and his adjutant sighed in unison. "Very well, Ben," Conway said, rising to his feet. "Keep looking for them, but remember we've got other problems to deal with."

"Yes, sir," Cohen said, and left, touching his hatbrim to Flora Conway, who was on her way into the captain's office.

It was immediately clear to Matt that Flora was unusually agitated. "It's Edwina, Warner," she said, confirming Matt's suspicion just as it was forming in his mind. "She's in tears, completely distraught. I had to get Maggie Cohen to help me."

Conway brought his chair forward. "Please, dear, have a seat," he offered, but she remained standing.

"Her husband has found out," she said, and bit her upper lip.

"Found out? Found out what?"

Flora looked at the two men in obvious astonishment. "Are you really so blind? Dennis Carter has found out that his wife and one of those boys—" She broke off abruptly as her face turned crimson.

"My God," Conway murmured, and he urged his wife into the chair and sat down himself.

"Warner, I think I can handle Edwina. I mean, I think the Carters will work it out. I don't know why I think that—but, well, anyway you'll have to talk to Carter. Edwina is really afraid of him."

"I'll certainly do so, my dear." Conway looked at Matt, who nodded his support.

167

"But Warner, those two boys must be sent to Regiment, or somewhere. Anywhere! But they have got to go. They've just got to go."

"My dear, I don't think there's any question about that." Rising, Conway reached for the brandy bottle and poured a drink for Flora, who accepted it gratefully.

"Which boy was it, Flora?" he asked when he sat down.

His wife looked across the room. "I don't know. I wonder if Edwina knows."

sixteen ───────────

Private George Gribble, once again walking his
post atop the east wall of Outpost Number Nine, watched
the first movement of light starting up behind the horizon.

It was still too dark to distinguish objects even close
to the post, though Gribble felt that he had seen something moving beyond the deadline. And yet, again, he
wondered if he perhaps was imagining it.

"They're out there," Sergeant Gus Olsen said, coming
up to the parapet to check on Gribble.

"Thought I saw somethin', Sarge," Gribble said.

"Don't think. Be sure," Olsen said, turning away.

Private Gribble continued to walk his post. It was as
he reached the tower just above the gate that he heard
something. He stood stock still, listening. Yes, definitely—from below, down by the gate.

Bringing his rifle down from his shoulder, Gribble
yelled, *"Halt!"*

He was greeted by silence, and was just about to fire in the direction of the sound when Sergeant Olsen came running up.

"It's down by the gate, Sarge."

Whipping out his Scoff, Olsen raced down the steps to the ground below. But there was nothing there. "Shit," he muttered to himself, holstering his handgun.

"Gribble," he called out to the sentry up on the parapet.

"Sarge!"

"Anything outside the wall?"

"Nothing, Sarge. Not a thing. But it's still pretty dark."

"Keep looking." Olsen had just started to turn away from the gate when his eyes caught something in the gray light. "Holy God!" he murmured as he saw that the gate was unlocked.

After locking the gate, he quickly went in search of Lieutenant Kincaid, who was already up and about.

"Got any idea who it might be?" Matt asked.

"I'd like to get my hands on the son of a bitch, whoever he is. Lieutenant, we can't be gettin' that careless, can we?"

"I don't think so, Sergeant."

"I mean, what with us all gettin' back from patrol and buryin' Fitzhugh and all that—do you think some stupid bugger just up and *forgot?*"

"Gribble told you he heard a noise, Sergeant."

Olsen's face looked his question, and then he asked it. "But . . . who, sir?"

"Have you seen the twins lately, Sergeant Olsen?"

Olsen's jaw fell to his chest, his eyes popped, and Kincaid left him in that condition, telling him to get more men on the wall to see if they could spot anyone outside.

He found Cohen in the orderly room. No, the first sergeant had not located the twins anywhere on the post.

"It's got to be them," Kincaid said when Conway joined them. "They hid until they felt they could make a break for it."

"All I can say is it's a damn good thing we found out before Mr. Lo discovered the gate was all nice and open for him."

All of them turned to the door as it opened fast and Windy Mandalian came in. "The place is crawlin' with hostiles, out past the deadline," he said. "Fox, Two Coyotes, and Long Horse and the Hunkpapas."

"If those twins are really out there—" Conway began.

"—they'll be greeted with open arms by Mr. Lo," Windy said, finishing the sentence.

"What do you mean?" Conway said.

"I mean they opened the gate not just to get out, but to let Fox and company in."

"How can you be sure of that, Windy?" Conway asked. "I know those two hated Yankees like poison, but this is going a bit far!"

"Not according to the company I was keeping in the wee hours of this morning." Windy said, grinning suddenly. "Cost me a bottle of redeye, which I will ask the United States Army to repay. No charge for my time, howsoever."

"Let's stop jawing here and get cracking," snapped Conway.

Kincaid swiftly checked the gate. There was still no sign of the twins, and for a moment he began to wonder if it really was them; but there was Windy's story.

Mr. Lo will be figuring the gate to be open, he was thinking, *and he'll try decoying us to the other walls.* He said as much to Carter, after disposing the platoons.

"We should be able to handle them easily with the Gatling, sir."

"The only trouble is that the old Medicine Gun, as

Mr. Lo calls it, is not very mobile. That's why we don't want them to know where it is."

He had noticed something about Carter: the man was even stiffer than usual, and yet there seemed something vague about him. Obviously what had happened had hit him hard.

Kincaid looked directly at him now. "Mr. Carter, the hostiles will be hitting us any minute now. I need every man I can get."

"I understand, sir."

"What I want to tell you, Dennis, is that each one of us is going to need every bit of himself for what's coming. No one can afford to be dreaming."

He saw Carter's eyes flicker. He had intentionally called him by his first name, which he had never done before.

"You can count on me to do my duty, Lieutenant Kincaid."

Matt heard the catch in his voice, and he realized that Carter was close to tears.

"Follow me," he said.

In a minute or two they had entered Kincaid's room in the bachelor officers' quarters. Matt went directly to a cupboard and brought out a bottle of whiskey. He poured a stiff shot and handed it to Carter.

"Drink this."

"Sir. I don't need Dutch Courage. I'm not afraid of the enemy."

"Maybe you don't need that drink, Mr. Carter, but *I* need you to drink it."

For a moment Carter looked as though he didn't understand, and Matt thought he might refuse again.

"This army out here," he said, looking at Carter dead center. "It's one place a man cannot indulge in either his pleasure or his pain."

Suddenly, Carter's face seemed to clear. In a steadier

voice, he said, "Thank you, sir. We don't need the drink now, sir."

"Put it down, then," Matt said with a nod. "We'll have it when it's over."

As they reached the parade, there came a shout from the tower, followed by rifle fire. In the dim light, some hostiles had tried slipping up to the gate.

Almost immediately the attack started. Fox, Two Coyotes, and Long Horse had split their forces into four groups, with three bands of mounted warriors charging in from the north, south, and west respectively. At the same time, a wave of warriors on foot started running in from the east, taking up prone positions in the sparse cover, shooting at the defenders along the ramparts. More braves followed them, also on foot, with pitch-soaked fire arrows notched and ready for firing.

The three mounted groups, each consisting of some twenty braves, hit their objectives at the same time, the Indians lying low across their horses' necks and firing at the defenders as they raced past with screams ripping the air.

From the eastern side the fire arrows arced high, trailing plumes of smoke into the parade, while other braves dropped to the ground and laid down a barrage into the men of First Platoon.

Matt trained his Colt on a young warrior who was running in with a fire arrow, leading him carefully before squeezing the trigger. The bullet tore into the warrior's abdomen, dropping him like a sack to the hard ground.

"They'll know now that we weren't surprised," he said to Windy, who was looking through his field glasses.

The scout brought the glasses down. "They figgered to slip inside 'fore sunup, no doubt. Jesus, it makes your hair stand up just thinkin' about it, huh?" But he said it as though he were discussing the weather, and Matt had to smile.

When Kincaid heard a shrill whinnying coming from the stables, he knew that some fire arrows must have struck there; the stables were always a main target in any attack. Looking down from the wall now, he saw there was fire at the gate, and smoke. The hostiles hoped to use this to cover their approach. But under the blistering fire from the men on the wall, they were forced to withdraw, leaving some fallen behind them. Carter's fire brigade began immediately throwing water on the gate and swatting at the flames with water-soaked blankets. But they were soon coughing helplessly from the smoke.

On the other sides of the post, the mounted braves had also withdrawn, and were regrouping to charge again. Now the warpainted ponies came at a dead run, while at the east wall the warriors on foot released a barrage of arrows. One soldier on the wall suddenly straightened, with a burning arrow in his head. Even before he fell, another hit him in the chest and his clothes were immediately on fire, as he crashed down into the parade. When the attackers raced away a second time, Conway shouted from the west wall that he had counted six riderless horses.

The hostiles had all withdrawn now beyond the deadline, but they had not given up, even though their casualties had not been few. Windy Mandalian was again watching through the glasses on the east wall.

"They're goin' to hit us on this side," he told Kincaid. "They been holding back about twenty riders."

"Sergeant Olsen!" Matt had spotted the First Platoon sergeant near the tower. "I want a casualty count!"

"Yessir!"

Matt turned to Carter. "Mr. Carter, check the stable for fire damage, and also see that the horses are saddled."

"Right, sir!"

"Any sign of those two boys, Windy?"

"Nope. And good riddance, I says."

"Here they come again!" The shout went up from the east wall, and Matt saw the mounted warriors racing in toward where he and the defenders of Outpost Number Nine were waiting. Other horsemen had joined them so that there was not only a first wave, but a second, and now even a third. The men on the parapet, firing in a staggered pattern, with half the men reloading while the others fired, were having to reload extra fast because of the third wave the hostiles were bringing in.

"Open the gate!" Kincaid shouted, running down the steps to the Gatling. "Let the bastards in!"

He saw the appalled looks on the faces of Carter and Olsen.

"Sergeant Olsen, get that gate open—and I mean right now! When I give an order, goddammit, don't think about it!"

He had reached the gun crew, and now shouted to Lieutenants Fletcher and Williams, "Second and Third Platoons, have half the men turn to fire at will on any hostiles who get inside!"

The gate swung open, and as the Sioux charged in, the Gatling swept a blizzard of lead into them. The attackers plunged from their horses, none of them getting more than a few feet inside.

"Roll it forward!" ordered Matt, and the men began pushing the big gun forward until it was right in the gate itself and spraying lead at the retreating Indians.

"Pull 'er back," Kincaid ordered. "And shut the gate!"

"I take it we're not going after them, sir," Carter said, coming up to Matt.

"Why not, Mr. Carter?"

"Ambush, sir. We'd be playing right into Mr. Lo's hands."

Matt suppressed the grin he felt by looking severely at his junior officer.

"Mr. Carter," he said, "the hostiles are drawing back. Take a mounted detail of three men and see what's lying out there. Be careful of any wounded who can still fire a gun. We'll cover you from here. You might take some prisoners."

"Yessir."

In a moment Carter and three men had mounted and were riding out to see at close hand the situation in the cleared land around the post.

Suddenly, when they were about a hundred yards out, but by now spread well apart, a shout went up from the wall.

"It's the kids! There they go!"

Olsen came hurrying along the parapet to where Kincaid and Windy Mandalian were watching the twins running across the open ground toward where the hostiles had retreated.

"They must've been hiding out by the paddock, Lieutenant," Olsen said.

The mounted detail had spread out further, and it was Carter who was closest to the boys. While the garrison watched, he kicked his horse into a gallop and raced after them.

"Jesus," muttered Windy. "If he kills those sons of bitches—which they deserve—his ass won't be worth a bucket of cold shit."

Matt was thinking the very same thing. Now both of them watched, helpless to do anything while Carter drew closer to the twins, who were running hard. He had his Scoff out, and now the three figures reached the perimeter and disappeared from view around a stand of crackwillow.

"Shit!" Mandalian lowered his glasses and spat. "Those boys ain't worth a box of prayers now, for sure."

Kincaid was already running down the steps, ordering horses and men to the gate. Firing could now be heard from beyond the stand of crackwillow. In minutes, Kincaid was pounding after Carter, with Olsen and half a squad of men behind him. The firing up ahead continued. And then it stopped abruptly as Kincaid galloped around the willow, a good bit ahead of the men following him.

A grim scene met him as he drew rein. Carter, his Springfield in his hands, was standing over the two boys, who were lying on the ground, covered with blood. They were dead. And Carter just continued to stand there looking down at them.

It was a moment before Matt noticed the three dead Indians lying just a few feet away.

seventeen ━━━━━━━━

"So Fox and Two Coyotes figured the boys crossed 'em. On account of the army came on so strong—*and* the gate was locked." Windy leaned back in his chair, looking for a place to spit.

Conway watched him with alarm, for he suddenly realized that someone had removed the cuspidor from the room. He was about to bellow for Corporal Bradshaw when the scout disengaged himself from his chair, ambled over to the window, and expectorated.

Conway simply looked at Kincaid, sighing in relief, while Matt smiled.

There was a loud knock at the door of the captain's office, and Sergeant Ben Cohen entered. He was carrying the brass cuspidor.

"What the hell?" Conway said.

"Them two, they went and hid it," Cohen explained. "Stretch Dobbs found it in the sutler's back room under a buffalo robe."

A silence fell upon them now. Then Conway looked up at his first sergeant.

"Sergeant, was Mr. Carter informed?"

"He was, sir. I believe he is on his way."

As he spoke, there was a second knock at the door. And this time it was Carter.

"Come in, Mr. Carter. Come in." Conway stood up and waved him to a chair. Then, reaching into his desk as Ben Cohen departed, he withdrew a bottle of whiskey.

"Matt, will you do the honors?"

All watched as Matt poured generous amounts for the men present.

Obviously, Carter was embarrassed. Indeed, Matt could see that he was at a loss as to how to handle this new approach by his senior officers.

"Sir, may I say something before you make a toast?" Kincaid asked.

"Of course."

"Mr. Carter, I notice that you are reporting to the commanding officer out of uniform. Explain it."

Carter looked as though he had been slapped.

"No excuse, sir."

"See that it doesn't happen again."

"Yes, sir. Sir?"

Kincaid cleared his throat, standing before his junior officer. "You are about to ask how you are out of uniform. Is that correct, Mr. Carter?"

"Yes, it is, sir. I was not aware . . ."

"Mister, remove that long blond hair from your shoulder."

It took only a second for the room to break into laughter. Carter was totally embarrassed as he plucked the strand of hair from his tunic.

Conway raised his glass. "Gentlemen, your health."

"And yours, sir!"

A short while and a few drinks later, Matt left the

Captain's office, and he realized that Carter had followed him.

"Sir, I want to thank you."

"Mr. Carter, that is not necessary."

"But sir, I really did want to kill them. And I might have, if the Indians hadn't suddenly appeared and done it for me."

"The Indians thought the boys had crossed them."

"I realized that later, sir."

"In the letter the captain is writing to Washington, he will say that you defended the boys with your life. Do you know why you tried to save them from Mr. Lo?" Kincaid asked.

"I don't know, sir."

They had reached officers' country again, after a turn around the parade.

"Sir, there is something I want to explain..."

Kincaid stopped dead in front of Carter. He had the impulse to touch him on the arm, but refrained. "No," he said. "I was there. I read the sign. What happened was good. But the best thing that happened was you didn't try to explain it." He was looking right into Carter's eyes. "Don't spoil it now."

Watch for

EASY COMPANY AND THE INDIAN DOCTOR

nineteenth novel in the exciting
EASY COMPANY series

Coming in August!

RIDE THE HIGH PLAINS WITH THE ROUGH-AND-TUMBLE INFANTRYMEN OF OUTPOST NINE— IN JOHN WESLEY HOWARD'S EASY COMPANY SERIES!